1440, WOMAN & DAGGER

A COLLECTION OF NOVELS

1440, WOMAN & DAGGER

A COLLECTION OF NOVELS

by Eddie Mikhail

Published by
The Word Connects
PO Box 737 Campbelltown NSW 2560 Australia
https://thewordconnects.com

Cover design and editing by the author.
Translated by the author.

ISBN: 978-1-923661-04-2
First Edition – 2026

Recommended for mature readers 18+ due to themes of violence and death.

For those who understand that moments shape lifetimes,
that love can wound and heal,
and that even in silence and darkness, the story continues.

TABLE OF CONTENTS

NOVEL I: 1440 1

1 3
2 5
3 9
4 12
5 14
6 18
7 23
8 30
9 32
10 35
11 38
12 40
13 44
14 47
15 54
16 60
17 63
∞ 66

NOVEL II: WOMAN 69

Reality 71

1- The Journey 72

2- The Friend 76

3- A Boy Is Born.. 79

4- The Principles Of Life 83

5- The Medal... 86

6- The Air 91

Fantasy.. 95

7- The Battle 96

8- The Survivor..101

9- The Encounter....................................... 105

When Reality Meets Fantasy 109

10- A Girl Is Born..110

11- The Warrior.. 113

12- The Tests..116

13- The Old Woman's Indoctrination 120

14- The Leader's Training...............................125

Present Moment.. 129

15- The Prison... 130

16- The Humiliation 134

17- The Second Encounter............................. 138

18- The Execution 143

19- The Nobody And The Queen..............................148

20- The Escape...152

    When Fantasy Parts With Reality 160

21- The Last War Against The Barbarians..................161

22- Inquiry About The Meaning Of Life 164

23- The Meeting That Is Destined To Be The Last.....168

    Reality 172

24- The Homeland 173

25- The Café 176

26- The Dagger...180

27- The Pottery..184

NOVEL III: DAGGER 191

Chapter One: The Dagger 193

Chapter Two: Hatred Manifestation.................... 205

Chapter Three: The Impossible Investigation............212

Chapter Four: Solving The Puzzle 220

Chapter Five: The Return Of The Dagger..................230

Chapter Six: The Detective's Case.......................237

NOVEL I
1440

For those who understand that
what we give in a moment can last forever.

1

You won't believe me if I tell you what happened to me today. Someone bumped into me on the street, and as soon as he saw me, he smiled broadly, then walked quickly towards me, grabbed me by the cheek and kissed me four times on the cheek.

He did it without warning, without any convincing reason. No, I had never seen him before in my life, and yes, I am absolutely certain of that. You want me to describe him to you! Very well, he looked like a young man in his early twenties, dressed like most young people of his generation, and he had a huge smile on his face from the moment I laid eyes on him. Even after he saw me, that smile did not disappear, but only widened.

That's all. After he left, I followed him with my eyes as he walked in the opposite direction until he disappeared completely. Then I turned and walked towards my house, dragging my heavy bag along the ground after a long, hard day at primary school, a smile on my face from what had just happened.

2

Since waking up, I had been weighed down by that trip. I had spent all the money I had on that new jacket, and I had to go to the savings office to withdraw five hundred pounds from my account to get through the rest of the month. I argued with my boss at work so that I could leave early, then headed straight to the post office, where I found a long queue waiting for me. I took my place at the end of the queue, of course. Then I stood waiting for my turn, and so I set my original Japanese Casio digital watch before my eyes and watched the seconds pass at a frightening speed before my eyes. Here was my life passing before my eyes, and the seconds became minutes, and the minutes became a quarter of an hour.

We all hate waiting; it makes us feel that our lives are slipping away before our eyes, despite ourselves, without us being able to do anything about it. Life is nothing but waiting. First, we wait for primary school to end, then we wait for secondary school, then high school, Then we wait for university to end, and from there we wait for national service to end, i.e. conscription, and from there we wait for work, we wait for love and then marriage, and some wait for marriage before love, we wait for children, and then we repeat the whole cycle of waiting with them, then we wait for retirement, and finally we wait for death.

Some wait for the day to end, some wait for the month to end, some wait for the year to end, and some wait for life to end. Everyone waits. Some wait for the bus, some wait for their loved ones on street corners and in casinos, some wait in line for bread, some wait for relief, some wait for the waiting itself, and some wait for the counting of money to end and their turn to receive their money. I was one of the latter.

How long had it been since he entered the place? I don't know, all I know is that I had reached the maximum possible state of boredom and weariness from waiting. I didn't notice him at first, except when he stared at me for a long time, then glanced at everyone in the place with long looks until he settled his gaze on me again, then turned to me, as if he had decided on something important with enthusiasm and energy.

"May I ask you a favour?" he asked.

"Go ahead," I replied.

"This notebook contains five thousand pounds. Take it, and here is my ID card, and here is my address on this small piece of paper and take that large envelope as well. In short," he said.

I want you to withdraw the entire amount from the cheque book, then take five hundred pounds from it, put the rest with the cheque book and the card inside the envelope, go to that address, and give it to my brother there. I would be very grateful for this great service."

"But why? Is one hour of your time worth five hundred pounds?!"

"I am in a real hurry and don't have a second to waste. Believe me, an hour is worth much more than that. Also, the money did not go to a stranger and was not misused. It went to my brother in humanity, who is you, of course.

"Don't you need a power of attorney or something like that to do this?"

"You're right, but I settled the matter amicably with the teller and completed the necessary legal procedures for you to withdraw the entire amount on my behalf. I referred you to him, so he knows your face and knows in advance what you are going to do," he explained.

"But five hundred pounds is a lot of money for such a trivial matter!" I protested.

"No, no, believe me, it's not a large amount at all. Just do me this favour and take it!" he said.

"All right, but tell me how you can trust me without even knowing my name?" I asked.

"You have bright eyes that show honesty, innocence and integrity, and a calm breathing rate that indicates kindness and peace in your heart," he replied.

"I could take all the money and leave, and yet you're not worried!" he said.

"I'm not worried at all. It's better for you to take the money than for it to stay here without any real use, and I'll forgive you for it too. Don't forget that money in this life is a means, not an end. There are much more important things that should occupy a person's mind," he said.

He paused to look me in the eye, then continued:

"Are you doing this for me?!"

"Yes, I am."

"Well, thank you. Thank you very much."

He waved goodbye and walked away quickly, leaving me immersed in a sea of surprise and confusion at this strange and bizarre behaviour, which I don't know whether to interpret as confidence, madness or insanity. In any case, I will wait, and I will be waiting anyways, and I won't have to withdraw a penny from my notebook. Now I will get the five hundred pounds without losing it from my notebook or losing its modest profits. All I have to do is wait, which is something I don't do, it just happens on its own, for none of us can stop the hands of time from continuing their eternal journey, in which they devour the life of man.

Time passed in a normal, routine manner until I reached the counter, then I did exactly what the young man asked me to do, took my commission, put the money, the card and the notebook in the envelope, went to that address, there, I gave the envelope to his brother and left for home, a faint smile on my face from that strange situation.

3

We taxi drivers deal with all kinds of people, believe me when I tell you this; we deal with misers, with generous rich people, with fools and wise people, with talkative people and silent people, with beautiful women who want to seduce us, and with courtesans who cannot find anyone of their level, with lovers, criminals, students, businessmen, with all kinds of people, and we have the opportunity to sit with them alone for a time that may be long or short.

Take, for example, the twenty-year-old young man who stopped me today. He stopped me and asked me to drive him around all day on his errands for five hundred pounds, and I agreed. How much do we earn in a day anyway? How long do we drive the streets aimlessly, expecting a customer on every corner? And when they haggle over the price and get on your nerves, even when the moment comes when you take the money, you blame yourself for working in this job and rebel against the existence of this type of people. Do they think I'm begging for charity or what?! Anyway, I accepted this job because it's secure, it changes the routine of my days, and it gives me a break from driving, which I thought I needed.

I opened my heart to this young man and told him my whole life story because I saw a calm smile on his face and he listened attentively with genuine interest. I told him my thoughts, and he agreed with me at first, then tactfully and wisely criticised some of the others. I told him about my problems and the bouts of rebellion and agitation that afflict me towards everything and anything. He advised me to take the easy solution that had always been before my eyes but which I had been blind to. Despite our long conversation, he did not talk much; I did. Nor did he tell me anything about his own problems or worries. It seemed as if he had devoted his life, or at least his day, to solving my problems. He seemed like a man without problems, or at least with problems that had been solved, or like a man bigger than his problems.

I loved this young man. He made me feel like I was his father and he was my son, because of his tenderness, love, wisdom and submission, which were accompanied by determination, strength, seriousness and manliness. No matter what I do, I will never forget him as long as I live. Even if sorrows, events, words, problems, and hardships pile up over my head over time, that young man will remain in a special, peaceful place in the recesses of my mind. Whenever I remember him, a smile is bound to appear on my face.

What made me tell you about that young man? I think it is one of those times when I will remember him, and whenever I remember him and talk about him, I will inevitably feel very happy, because then I know that the world is still fine and that there are still some good men in it.

"Taxi. The big shopping mall, please?"

"Twenty pounds?"

"Fifteen?" I asked.

"Goodbye, pal," he replied.

"Didn't I tell you?"

"Do you believe me now?"

"What's wrong with these bastards?"

4

I was about to finish my prayers when I caught sight of him out of the corner of my eye. He entered quickly, pushing through the crowd, indifferent to them, until he stopped, raised his hands high and started praying. He stood praying for a long time, and his face showed every expression that a human face can show. At times he looked happy, at other times sad, at times energetic, at times listless.

He was shouting, crying, wailing, lamenting, begging, and pleading. He kept his eyes closed most of the time, but when he opened them, he did not seem to notice anyone else in the place, and he certainly did not notice me. In any case, I am used to no one noticing me. Who would notice an old man like me, over seventy years old? To be honest, I was surprised to see that young man, who was twenty or more years old, because I noticed that the house of worship today is frequented only by men and women of an old age—like me—who have experienced everything in life and know exactly what it is worth. Nothing, and the children who have not yet experienced anything in life, few of the young people I see in the house of worship.

This young man prolonged his prayer anyway, it exceeded an hour, and I was embarrassed by how much I was staring at him. I wanted to leave, as it was time, and... So I left, leaving that young man behind, full of curiosity about him, my mind filled with a perplexing question that would remain unanswered. When would he finish his prayer and leave?

5

Everyone has a story, except me.

This dignified man loves his three-year-old daughter so much that he buys her a toy once a week, as one of the ways he tries to win her affection.

That child loves to buy sweets from my shop every day, whenever he has the opportunity and the money. His greatest ambition is to have five pounds to buy a large bag of crisps and a huge bar of luxury chocolate. For this child, my shop is the best place in the world simply because it is the only place he knows near his home that sells sweets, and he thinks about going to my shop all the time.

Then there is the boy who buys notebooks to write his lessons in, and the gloom is as clear as day on his face; because the holidays are over and school is starting, which means memorising lots of lessons, carrying a heavy bag, waking up early, going to bed early, no TV, no playing, and so on and so forth. .

And then there is the man who buys special pens of a specific type and high quality, and high-purity paper, which he seems to need for his work, which relies heavily on writing; he may be a writer, a poet, a journalist, or something else. and that man is accustomed to buying his supplies from my shop, so it is clear that it has become a habit that he does not intend to give up.

And there is that boy who passes by me every day arm in arm with his girlfriend, and that boy who passes by me every day on his way to school, and that girl who passes by the shop every Tuesday on her way to maths class at her friend's house at the end of the street, and that young man who exercises every day, running past the shop on his way to the gym...

Everyone has a story, but I don't.

After I became a pensioner, my wife died after a long illness, and my children got married and entered the grind of life, the whirlwind of days, and the squeeze of years. My companions left, my friends disappeared, and life seemed empty, barren, meaningless and worthless, after all I had seen and known of it. I felt it telling me clearly that I was no longer of any use to this world, so I should wait for my time in silence, without noise, complaint or question.

And so, I complied with what life was telling me, and I stayed in my shop day and night, watching the people around me, just living, contemplating the lives of many, but without a life of my own to live. I watch, I observe, I see, but I do not act, interact, or live. I am not saying that I have experienced everything, only that I am a man who has experienced life.

Today I witnessed a story that was unique in its strangeness, and I even participated in it. It has been a long time since I have seen anything like this story in its strangeness. I thought nothing could ever surprise me anymore. A young man came to me today and asked to buy a blow-up jumping horse toy from the front window of the shop, so I took the key and went to open the window.

"Do you know that that toy has been in that display case for twelve whole years?" he asked.

I looked at him in surprise, for what he said was true. Even when I renovated the shop, I did not renovate that display case or change its contents, and throughout all those years, no one had bought that toy. So, in amazement, I asked him:

"How do you know that?" I asked.

"I had that game when I was a child. I loved it very much, but one day one of my child guests broke it, and then I forgot all about it. After I grew up and entered the second year of secondary school, I passed by your shop one day and saw it. I wanted to buy it, but I was too embarrassed to do so, as it is not appropriate for adults to play with such childish games. So, I postponed buying it until tomorrow, then the next day, then the next day. Because I passed by your shop every day on my way to school and on my way to visit my best friend, I got used to seeing it and wishing to buy it, then changing my mind every day.

Years passed, and whenever I visited my friend, I would see your shop and remember the game. Finally, the day came when I decided to buy the game, and when I went to buy it, I saw that it was a wonderful symbol in its place, a symbol of the near and the far at the same time, something that catches the eye but cannot be held in the hand. So, I decided to leave it alone, but today I decided to buy it, after two years at school, five years at college, three years of military service, and two years of work. I even decided to tell you everything I told you, so that you could bear witness to the story of that toy."

With great surprise from a man who had been melted and amazed by life, I opened my mouth to speak at length and eloquently, and said:

"One and a half pounds!"

He gave me two pounds and then hurried away.

Does the story need commentary? I don't think so.

6

What brought you here?! Couldn't you find a better place to spend your day than this awful place?! Couldn't you find anyone else to sit with, you poor wretch?! It's clear that you have nowhere to go, no one to talk to, nothing to do, no work to accomplish, and that you are suffering from a terrible emptiness.

I, my friend, am completely paralysed, which makes me unable to speak or move, unable to move a single muscle in my body, unable even to close or open my eyes. There are those who close them for me in the evening when it is time to sleep, which I do not have the luxury of determining myself, as I am unable to make any facial expressions to indicate what I want. There are also those who open them for me in the morning, also at a specific time.

Of course, you can imagine that I do not receive any visitors. Who would want to visit an inanimate object that breathes? To my family, I have become like a chair or a table, like any piece of furniture they used to use every day, but which has now lost its function.

Some people use the excuse that they refuse to see me in this state, so they sold me and sold my cause, using a foolish excuse. I have accepted this fate and am trying to live with it. If they truly love me, they must also accept it and try to live with it. Others come to visit me once a year for a very short visit without words, to ease their conscience. My family, friends and loved ones have left me, and I am alone.

All I have are my thoughts during the day and my dreams at night. I can hear and see, but I cannot even move my eyeballs. This is how you see me, lying on the bed with my eyes open, staring at the ceiling with no expression on my face, the tube that supplies me with glucose extended from my hand.

That is why I was surprised by your visit, but in any case, I am glad you came, and I am also glad you listened to my thoughts; few can hear thoughts, my friend. I wish I could offer you something, but you know I cannot even speak, so please help yourself!

Look, my roommate has a visitor. How lucky I am! Today I will see something different from what I am used to. I saw the visitor, who looked like a young man in his early twenties. He entered the room with a huge bouquet of roses and a package that looked like a gift. He rushed to his friend, kissed him, left the roses on the bed, and then said, "I brought you this," and handed him the package he was holding. His sick friend opened the package and said, "What is this?!" "It's that book," he replied.

"I brought you this," he said, handing him the package.

"What is this?!" his sick friend replied as he unwrapped the paper.

"It's that book you asked me to borrow the other day. I bought it for you."

"Wow!! Unbelievable! I asked you for that book over a year ago. I forgot, my friend," he said.

"Better late than never," his friend replied.

He sat up straight and began to flip through the pages of the book, and his visiting friend asked him:

"Did you get it after you asked me for it?"

"No, you know it's a really rare book and also very expensive," he answered.

The visitor smiled, and...

Auh, aii, ahhhh, aaaa.

I am in pain, and the worst part is that I cannot protest or even express my disgust, because people see me as I am, while a volcano rages inside me. I did not know how long I had been in pain, but now the visitor is leaving.

I didn't know why he stopped in front of my bed! Why he looked at me like that! Why he picked up the report on my condition that was hanging on the bed! Why he read it with such interest! Why he left so affected! I continued to be in pain even after he left, and...

The nurse came and stuck that needle in me, and left with surprising efficiency, as if she were a robot, but I felt better after she left. It seems that the machines connected to my body told them that I was suffering from some kind of problem. That's good, that's good.

I'll try to get some sleep, but how can you sleep with your eyes open?! I'll have to wait until nightfall. Damn this! Damn, damn, damn. Leave me alone for a while so I can calm down....

....

What brought that young man back?! I mean the visitor who visited my roommate. This time he's coming towards me with a large bouquet of flowers in his hand, which he places where I can see it, and with a huge smile he runs his hand through my hair, then kisses my forehead, and then leaves, saying:

"I'll be back in a little while," he said.

He didn't take long, and when he returned, he didn't come back empty-handed. He brought a television and a video player, plugged them in, placed them where I could see the screen, then approached me slowly and whispered:

"What would you like? What are your viewing preferences?"

He turned on the television and slowly changed the channels, trying to read my eyes to see what I wanted. When he failed, he settled on a channel he thought I might like, and I did indeed like it.

"Don't worry, mate, we'll make your days better. Believe me, there are people out there who are worse off than you, and you know that. I'll film whatever you want with the video camera. Your home, your family, your friends, whatever you want. Just hang in there, my friend, and think positive thoughts, because people create their thoughts, and then their thoughts create them. All you have to do, my friend, is adopt a positive idea. Just adopt it and believe in it, and it will do the rest. I wish I could spend more time with you, but I have other things to take care of."

Then he left.

Should I tell you, my friend, that today is the happiest day of my life? Yes, I will tell you. All I really needed was a touch of tenderness. Why do people always care only about themselves, their food, their drink, their possessions, their money, and their happiness, forgetting everything about others? And why did everyone who knew me before that damn accident turn away from me? What happened has happened, so stop your disgust and pity, and treat me this way. Your disgust won't change anything. That boy did the right thing. I hope to see you again, lad. I will pray to God to see you again.

I looked at my companion in the room, and he seemed stunned by what he had seen from his friend. His view of me will be different from before. It will definitely be different.

7

Today my uncle came to our house, and that boy came with him, holding his arm. He shook my hand, while my uncle asked me to get dressed, because they wanted me to go on an important trip. So, without asking any questions, I got dressed and the three of us left.

When I asked my uncle what was going on, he told me that the boy wanted to tell me something very important. So, ten minutes later, I found myself sitting alone with him at a table in a casino overlooking the river, while my uncle was busy reading his newspaper at another table only five metres away from us.

A minute later, we ordered two glasses of lemonade, and after a few moments of silence, he spoke:

"Good morning, miss. Do you remember me? I hope you do. We have only exchanged a few words, such as 'good morning', 'good evening', 'excuse me, I'd like to pass', 'how are you', 'thanks God'. Those were the only words we exchanged, but despite this, I would like to tell you something very important."

"Go ahead," I said with interest.

"We met for the first time when I was five years old. I saw you then and recognised you. I recognised you from your gaze, your behaviour, your great love for all your friends, your lack of jealousy, hatred or envy towards any of your peers, your warm, comforting smile, your calm, beautiful clothes, your long, soft brown hair, your wide, clear honey-coloured eyes, and your pure, white skin," he said.

His tone grew even more tender as he continued:

"From your gait, when you walk, everyone who sees you is convinced that you never touch the ground because you are so delicate, but rather that you fly at least two inches above the ground. From your greeting, you resemble a butterfly whose beauty and delicacy make one afraid to touch it for fear of harming it. You resemble a delicious biscuit, delicate in texture, extremely soft, and so white that a man would be afraid to touch it for fear of leaving his fingerprints on its bright colour or breaking it because of its extreme delicacy," he continued.

I contemplated this strange and wonderful candour, and he continued:

"I have seen you grow up before my eyes over the years, and with each passing day you become more beautiful, in your character, your nature, your spirit and your appearance. I have heard you speak and express yourself, and I knew that your opinions are the same as mine. I saw you talking and interacting with those around you with kindness, gentleness, and love, mixed with strength, determination, and wisdom," he continued.

Then pain appeared on his face as he continued:

"Sometimes life is hard on us. Those we trust with our secrets betray us, some reject us just merely for our looks, people hate us for trivial and illogical reasons after a long time, true friends neglect us, claiming they are busy, and people leave us as soon as the stage that brought us together ends; school, college, army, work, life, as if we had come into this life to say goodbye and part with people, not to meet them."

A note of melancholy crept into his voice as he continued:

"We spend long nights of loneliness, anxiety, terror and fear, with our studies, books, paper and pens. We are afraid, we despair, depressed, frustrated with people, with the world, with our mistakes, with our narrow-mindedness, with our lack of education, with our ignorance of wisdom, with our limited capabilities, with our shortcomings and our enormous ambitions. We shut ourselves in our rooms, we wonder, we punch the walls with our fists until they bleed, we fill our papers with random, strange, sick shapes and drawings."

Then a smile appeared on his lips as he continued:

"Amidst all the pains of life, when loneliness is the vehicle, despair is the road, escape is the method, and the destination is destruction, and when there is no escape, I see your face and say that there is something beautiful and happy waiting for me in this life, so I will live to wait for it. How many situations have I faced in which you were with me, with your kindness, your imagination, your face, your presence, your existence!"

He gazed into the distance, as if looking at the past with eyes that transcended time, and continued:

"I would not have been able to finish my studies if you had not been in my mind and heart, telling me: Work hard to finish your studies so you can get a job, and you will find me waiting for you! Just work hard, and when I finished, I had to wait again until I finished my military service, then wait until I got a job, then earn enough money to buy an apartment, furnish it, and decorate it. Long years of struggle, I didn't want you to be with me. Your family would not tolerate me, and you yourself might not be able to wait for me. Even if you could, I would be doing you an injustice, because you might find someone better than me who is ready to marry you if you did not know me. That is why I decided not to let you know how I felt."

I asked him:

"But why didn't you tell me how you felt before and then leave me free to choose whether to accept or reject you?"

"It never occurred to me to approach you, for you seemed to me like an ancient holy ground, as old as the earth itself, placed atop the highest peak in the world, reserved for the elite of humanity throughout history. Therefore, the idea of approaching you always terrified me before it approached my mind," he replied.

"So why are you telling me this now?!" I asked him in confusion.

"Ah. I'll tell you why. Some things have become clear to me recently," he replied quickly.

"I'm telling you now because the past is gone and we can't change it. All we can do is make our present good so that our future past will be good. The present moment will be the past in just a second, and as for the future, it is all in the hands of the Creator, and no creature can guarantee it. All we can do is hope for a better future that we do not know and cannot guarantee," he continued quickly.

He opened his palms in front of his face and continued:

"All we have is the present, the moment. The moment you are living now is your life. The past is a memory that has ended, and the future is not guaranteed. Life is like a night, as they say, and if life is the night, not yesterday or tomorrow, then I have decided to live my whole life now, and I will not put off my whole life until tomorrow, for it is not guaranteed, as I told you before. Rather, I will live every day, every moment, as if it were my whole life, and I will never put off living again," he said.

Then he said in a tone of that who is ending his speech:

"I loved you, my dear. I have always loved you, and I have never stopped loving you. I saw you in every story I read, in every film I watched, in every song I heard. I loved you without knowing anything about you. What do you study? Do you work? Do you have children? Are you married? Are you engaged? Do you love someone? Whatever your answer, I wanted to tell you what I'm telling you now, so that you know that someone has loved you with all this love!"

Then he bowed his head, as if waiting for an answer...

And...

"Well! What do you think of what you've heard?" he asked.

I noticed something important and asked, "Wait. Does my uncle know all this?"

He shook his head and said, "No, no. I've known your uncle well for a long time, but life took us away after it let us down and distracted us from each other."

"This morning, I called a friend of mine and got your uncle's phone number, which I had lost, and then I called him and told him that I wanted to talk to you about something important that couldn't wait a moment longer. Because of his absolute trust in me, he set up this meeting so that I could tell you what I wanted to say in a suitable atmosphere," he explained.

"So, my uncle does not know what you just told me!" I said, relieved that my uncle did not know about the matter.

He nodded his head and said, "Yes. Your uncle knows nothing."

After a moment of silence, he asked, "What do you think about what I just said?"

I looked away from his wide, piercing eyes that seemed to penetrate my soul and said:

"Give me until tomorrow to think about what you've said, and we'll meet here at the same time," I said.

He looked very disappointed, as if I had said no to him. Did he expect me to throw myself into his arms as soon as he told me how he felt about me? I didn't know what to say to him after seeing the sadness in his eyes, so he said:

"Anyway, I wanted to tell you how I feel, just so you know... and..."

I noticed his confusion, so I said:

"But I didn't reject you," I clarified.

"Nor did you accept me," he quickly replied.

"One has to think about it," I said, with a little annoyance and a lot of confusion.

"And sometimes you have to use your intuition and make a quick decision. At least tell me how you feel about me," he said with confidence in the truth of what he was saying.

I paused for a moment, searching for the right words, and then finally said, "Well, I like you, and... and... that's all I can say right now."

He looked at me with love and tenderness in his eyes, then said something I didn't understand at all:

"Okay, the next time I see you, don't forget what I told you today!"

I agreed to this strange request, and...

"Okay."

I agreed, and he put his hands on the table, ready to leave, saying:

"Goodbye for now... Can I call you my love, just for today?"

I thought for a moment, then nodded my head shyly in agreement. He stood up, flew away with joy, and said:

"You cannot imagine how much happiness you have brought to a heart that has been longing for this moment since birth. Goodbye, my love," he said.

He greeted me, shook hands with my uncle, then hurried away. My uncle came to me and...

"What did he want from you, my dear?" he asked.

".......

And we left.

8

It is very rare for a student to leave a letter for his professor, but I think we are living in a time of wonders, because that student left a letter addressed to his thesis supervisor for me to deliver to him, which I did.

"Here you are, Professor. This letter is for you," I said.

"From whom?" the professor asked me.

"From that student whose thesis you are supervising from..." I replied.

"Yes, yes," he said.

He took it from me and placed it on his desk to read it later at his leisure, but...

What's stopping you from reading it? You are the one who decides what to do with these pages, and you have the right to do as you please. So, if you don't want to read it, move on to the next chapter, and if you want to read it, go to the next line...

My dear Professor:

I offer you my sincere and abundant greetings...

This letter is from your brilliant student, whom you loved and nurtured academically, socially, and morally, and whose graduation project you supervised, and whose master's thesis you are supervising.

I know, my dear teacher, that you see me as your best student, the bright and hard-working one, but I would like to clarify something to you, which is that I fell short during my years of education. Throughout all of them, I did not study well from the beginning of the academic year but rather wasted my precious time on things that were of no use or benefit. That is why I regret every second I wasted in the past, and I wish I could turn back time to make the best use of my time as I would like to now.

I just wanted to tell you that if I could go back six years, I would do things differently and better than I did before. I would have turned all my good and very good grades into near-perfect ones, and I would have engraved all the knowledge in my mind like my name. That is all I wanted to tell you.

Thank you very much, my dear teacher.

9

"Sixty years ago, the German scientist Max Planck attempted to describe the phenomenon of radiation emission from radioactive materials using a general law. He arrived at a strange conclusion and announced that he had discovered a law from which it could be deduced that energy is not emitted in a continuous stream, but in indivisible bursts called quanta," he said.

The professor cleared his throat and was about to continue the lecture, but he seemed to remember something, so he cleared his throat again, then began coughing violently. Many of the students murmured, and among them I recognised the voice of the person sitting next to me.

"Look who's come to the lecture!" he said.

I was really surprised to see the person standing at the door, as he was a very dear friend of mine who had left college and was now busy with his new life. I wondered what had brought him here!

"With your permission, Professor?" he asked.

"Go ahead!" the professor replied.

Our friend at the door asked for permission and now he's coming towards the row we're sitting in to sit next to me, and he did, so I shook his hand warmly, and...

"Planck explained that sunlight, like any other radiation emitted from a radiant source, consists of small bursts of energy, and that the reason light and heat appear to us as a continuous stream is that these amounts of energy are so small that our senses cannot distinguish between them," the Professor continued.

"But what made you think of me, my friend, to come here and attend a lecture that you attended three years ago?!" I asked.

"I always wanted to visit you, but I always told myself that I was too busy. Recently, however, I realised that people have all the time in the world and that they do what is most important to them first and, in their spare time, do what they enjoy most. So, I asked myself, 'Am I going to let the whirlwind of life take me away and distract me from my true friends?' The answer was no."

"I'm touched, my friend. Thank you."

"Planck also explained that these small amounts of energy are not equal but vary with the wavelength of the radiation. The amounts of energy emitted by red light are smaller than those emitted by blue light, and the amounts emitted by blue light are smaller than those emitted by X-rays."

That's how friendship should be. It lasts for years, unburdened by the passage of time, problems, concerns, work, home, wife and children, but remains for life. I turned my gaze to my friend sitting next to me, then turned my head back to face the professor to listen to the rest of the lecture.

"Experiments have proven Planck's theory to be correct, leading to its continued success and significant scientific advances in the 20th century," the Professor added.

10

The files piled up on my desk, and I didn't know how long it would take me to finish them. I wondered if whoever put them there thought I would be able to finish them in a single day! It didn't matter, because it was almost lunchtime anyway, with only fifteen minutes left, and I certainly wouldn't be able to finish all this work in those few minutes. So, I closed my eyes, covered my face with my hands, buried my head in them, and rested my elbows on the desk.

Then my mind started thinking about the clothes my six-year-old son had asked for, then about school expenses, then about my wife's new pregnancy expenses, then about the doctor my sick mother needed, and finally about my damn manager who asked for time to think when I asked him for an advance. Of course...

I jumped in fright when I felt a hand on my shoulder. I looked up and stared at the owner of the hand, which only increased my fear. Believe me, if it had been Dracula himself, I wouldn't have been so scared, because this was the real

Dracula, not the fictional Dracula from fantasy novels, but the teacher who taught Dracula how to suck the blood from his victims, get the most out of them, and leave them dead, useless for anything else. The person whose face you saw is my manager, and...

"You sleep at work, with all this work in front of you, and you are late for work, as you were last Tuesday, and you lose the company's clients, like the client you lost last January, and you are absent without permission, like that day ten months ago when you were absent, and with all this negligence, you want an advance! I'll be waiting for you in my office after work."

And with that, he left without even giving me a chance to respond. After he had spewed all his venom, I was filled with resentment and anger. This bastard remembers every mistake I've made in the last five years. When the fire inside me flared up, I saw him.

I didn't know what he was talking about, why he had come to me now, or why he hadn't waited for me to return from work to visit me at home, but I put all those thoughts aside and got up to greet him.

"How are you, man?"

"How are you?"

"I'm fine."

"Me too. I'm honoured by your visit, my friend."

"May God keep you safe, man, but I apologise for coming without an appointment, and to your workplace. That's why I chose to come during your lunch break, and I won't keep you long."

"Don't say that, man. What's up?"

"You asked me for money not long ago, and at the time I intended to buy some necessities, but after thinking about it,

I realised that you needed the money more than I did, and that the things I wanted to buy were not that important and could be postponed. I was selfish when I refused, so here is the money."

He handed me the money. I took it, looked down, then counted it, and found it to be double what I had asked for, so I said:

"But this is too much, man."

"Don't worry about it, pay me back when you can, I won't ask you about it, I don't need it right now," he replied.

"I don't know what to say!" I exclaimed.

"Don't say anything. There's nothing to say between friends," he said.

There was silence, and the silence lingered, then he spoke:

"I was afraid you would be embarrassed by me at home, so I came to you at work, on neutral ground, to avoid any awkwardness."

"You're right. I would have been embarrassed, and I wouldn't have taken it from you," I replied.

Silence continued for a while, then he broke it:

"I'll leave you to your meal. Goodbye."

"Goodbye," I replied.

And so, he left, leaving me in my confusion. Did I mean so much to him that he would give up all that money, not knowing when he would get it back, and give up the things he wanted to buy for me? What kind of friend is this? He is a true friend, definitely a true friend.

11

"One lux, one regular, two lentils, and three tagines."

You are inside a famous kushari restaurant in that popular neighbourhood, and I am the waiter who brings the dishes to the customers' tables, and you found me at our peak time. In fact, all our times are peak times, as the restaurant never runs out of customers, and you even find them waiting outside until some of those who fill all the seats in the restaurant leave.

The truth is that many come from far away just to eat at our restaurant. In short, I'm busy right now. Can you come back later, maybe after three lines?

Good, well done, now I can talk to you with a clear mind. So, what did you want to tell me? Let it be... But don't you think you're asking for too much this time? No need, I'll take care of it. No, don't worry. Yes, yes, no. I told him repeatedly not to do it, but he did it anyway. He ignored my words and did what he wanted, despite everyone's objections. No, don't tell me to calm down. You don't know anything, and neither do you...

Wait! Do you see that boy? Yes, the one sitting at the table at the very end. See how he eats?! He eats as if he's in love with the dish. He sucks up the pasta, then plays with it with his tongue, dancing with it with his incisor teeth, which he brings to his molar teeth, which embrace it with strange tenderness, and he tastes the tomato sauce, lentils and fried onions with indescribable pleasure. He also chews the rice in his mouth with unusual ecstasy, eating very slowly and deliberately, so much so that you would think it would take hours before he finishes half the dish.

Yes, and what proves his great enjoyment of the dish is that he closes his eyes. Who closes their eyes while eating?! In all my years of work, I have never seen anyone eat with such appetite! What is wrong with this boy?! Why is he doing this?! Let's get back to our topic. Where did we leave off? Ah, yes, you don't know anything about him, so don't say anything...

12

"Slope arms!" he barked, dragging out the command.

"One, two, three, four! One, two, three, four!"

And so, we stood there training, and when the training time was over, the day went on like any other day. After we had lunch, it was time for our daily short break, and less than fifteen minutes into the break, that soldier came to me and told me that the commander wanted me. I rushed to the commander's office in a hurry, with a thousand thoughts running through my mind.

What did I do? What did I do wrong? What did I fail at? Did I, did I, did I? When I reached him, I saluted him, and he looked away from me after a glance that lasted a fraction of a second, and...

"Are you...?" "Yes, sir." "You have an important phone call. Take your time, no one will disturb you."

In a daze, I went to the phone, picked up the receiver, and...

"Hello, hello. Who is this?" I asked.

"Don't you recognise me? Shame on you, man."

"Just remind me who you are."

"Okay, sir," I replied.

"Unbelievable, what made you think of me now?!" he asked.

I recognised him immediately from the way he said "sir".

"I wanted to talk to you about something important," he said.

"It must be really important, if it made you call me here," I replied.

"It's important to me," he said.

"How did you manage to contact me anyway?!" I asked.

"I asked all my friends, acquaintances and relatives if they could help me contact you, until I found a friend who knows a general. I asked him to contact you, and he agreed. He called the commander of your unit, and that was it."

"Wow! You did all that just to talk to me?! You should have just called me at home during my leave, man."

"It's better to be early, man, and I needed to talk to you now."

"Okay! What is it?!"

"I wanted to ask for your forgiveness."

I continued to listen to him, and I was stunned by what I heard, so I interrupted him and commented on what he was saying as he continued:

"I have spoken ill of you, gossiped about you, belittled you repeatedly, and told many people how opportunistic and selfish you are, how you love yourself more than any other creature, and how you exploit everything and everyone in your path to serve your own purposes, how you suck it dry until there is nothing left, then you throw it aside, how you take the easy way out and don't do ordinary things yourself, but leave them to others out of laziness or lack of self-confidence, how you are materialistic and covetous of other people's money, possessions, skills and abilities, abusive, a gossip, empty-headed and a womaniser. Forgive me, my friend; I have condemned you many times in my heart.

I paused for a moment.

"Did you call to tell me what you just said?!" I asked.

"Yes," he replied.

"And what do you expect me to say?!" I asked. Or rather, what do you want me to say?!"

"That you forgive me," he said.

"Actually, I'm very confused, and everything is mixed up. How about we postpone this conversation until I return?" I replied.

"No, no, no, that's not possible. Let's finish it now. All I want to hear from you is one word: I forgive you," he insisted.

"I have never found anyone who was genuine in telling the truth as it is to me as much as you did today. You went to great lengths to contact me today, but you are my friend! My friend! You should have told me what you were thinking from the beginning, but you know what, I would not have listened. Now I'm telling you this. I will think about everything you've said to me and take it into consideration to improve myself and my behaviour. I forgive you for everything you say you did and said."

"You forgive me?!"

"Yes, I forgive you."

Thank you very much, my dear friend.

You're welcome, but I don't think what I did deserves to be acknowledged in this way and in such a hasty manner. Stop thinking that way, adopt positive thoughts about me, let me know later about the things that bother you about me, don't say those things about me again to other people, love me and stop criticising me in your mind, and why on earth didn't you wait for me to come back?!

"Who can guarantee tomorrow, my friend?"

"No one. Anyway, I'm glad you called, and that I heard your voice, which I haven't heard in a long time."

"I'm very glad that I found you, and that I told you what's in my heart, my friend."

"Good."

"Well then, goodbye, my friend."

"No. Don't say that. Say see you later, man."

"But you won't be back for at least a week."

"So what? Let's meet then, and let's say now I'll see you then."

"Goodbye, my friend."

Beep.

He hung up before I could say goodbye.

For the rest of the day, I replayed our conversation once, twice, three times, and found myself loving and appreciating that dear friend even more. Then it was time for dinner.

13

"Did the supervisor scold you again?" he asked.

"Yes, Father," I replied.

"Why?" he demanded.

"I ruined the work," I admitted.

"Why? Why can't you do something simple the right way?" he pressed.

I bowed my head in front of my father in the living room, then he continued:

"You will get fired from your job, which will lead to..."

"Ring, ring, ring!"

The doorbell.

I got up to open the door, glad for the interruption, and when I did, I found, I found, I found, I found... Ah! It was that friend. I shook his hand and invited him in, and when the four of us were alone, just him and me and two cups of tea.

"I have come to tell you all the tricks of the trade, so listen to me carefully..." he said.

And he began to speak in a structured, numbered, important, concise and useful manner, words you will not find in books, practical knowledge gained through trial and error, practice and years of experience.

I don't know why he told me everything he knew! That way, he would be no different from me, we would compete with each other, and I would affect his profits. When I told him what I was thinking in surprise, he replied simply:

"As the saying goes, my friend, don't give me a fish, teach me how to fish, and that's what I did. I have done good, and God does not forget such things. God will increase the giver, and hiding information or benefits from people is a great evil, for by doing so you harm people with your sin, and what you do not use to benefit people will be taken from you. Likewise, when I tell you this, you will not forget me and you will benefit me one day, and you will be grateful to me, and I will not forget the information I have told you. Only information that is not used is forgotten. When I tell you this, I am using it, and if I happen to forget the information I have told you, I will find someone to remind me of it. I also feel great happiness in giving, which is unlike any other happiness. Are the reasons I have given you sufficient, or do you want more?"

"No. That's enough, but I just don't know how to thank you. By covering your observations, I won't ruin any work anymore," I replied with a broad smile.

"Come with me now for half an hour, so we can confirm our information with practical application in the workshop," he said.

I tried to dissuade him. I insisted, and he insisted, and in the end we went, and I tried it with my own hands, and the work was not ruined, but came out with strange precision. When we finished after a quarter to an hour and, I thanked him again, and he went on his way, while I stayed in the workshop practising what I had just learned, full of questions.

Why did he come to me now? Why did he tell me everything without exception, leaving nothing for himself to distinguish himself? Why did he so easily give me what he had acquired through hardship, toil, and a long time? I found no answer except that he undoubtedly loved me. There is no other explanation! Don't you see that?

14

"I love you, I love you, I love you," he said.

He touched my hand when I flinched and quickly backed away, quickly averting my eyes from his deep eyes, and looking in every direction when my eyes met his.

Standing far away, he stared at me steadily, his arms crossed behind his back, his head thrown back to reveal the stubble on his chin. I flinched, then shivered, and said to my companion:

"Excuse me for a moment!"

"Go ahead!" he said.

I got up quickly and went to him. I left the one who was sitting with me, professing his love, and went to where the other one was standing far away. Without greeting him, or saying a word, or making any introductions, I asked him:

"Did you come for me?" I asked.

"Yes, I came for you, and... good evening, by the way," he replied.

"Good evening," I said.

I bowed my head to the ground, then asked him, pointing to the table where my companion was sitting, who had told me he loved me less than a minute ago:

"What do you want me to do with him?" I asked.

"Ask him to leave and come back tomorrow at the same time, as something urgent has come up that you can't tell him about now," he replied.

Two thoughts crossed my mind: the first was that 'you had calculated everything', and the second was 'why don't you do this and leave now?' But I used the first one, and he laughed, then I went to send the person who confessed his love to me away, and when I was done, I went to standing guy, and...

"Huh! What do you want?!"

A question like that comes from a girl he loved for two years, then tells him that he is nothing more than a brother to her, enough to make everything he thought he would say to her fly out of your mind, and all he can say is: All I want to say to you is goodbye, but he asked:

"I came to ask you just one question. Why did you leave me?" he asked.

"Did you come here now, after all this time, to ask me that question?!" I asked.

"You never answered it," he said.

"I did answer you," I replied.

"A superficial, unsatisfactory answer. I want the truth, the whole truth," he said.

"Honesty hurts," I replied.

"When you hold a knife and stab someone, it won't hurt them more if you tell them the real reason for the stab, but it will help them to be cautious in the future. What difference would it make if the reason was theft, or just murder, or madness, or anything else?"

"Look, you're a good person, but do you think you'll be admired by billions of girls around the world? Of course not. Every man has a certain group of girls who think similarly to him. A thief will not settle for someone with your morals; she will settle for a thief. Consider what happened to you as an experience that failed, and that's it. Forget about it, leave it behind you, and let it be a reason to make you stronger. Don't think about it anymore."

"All I want is the reason," he said.

"You're not my type, you're not right for me, you're not the man of my dreams," I replied.

"Then why were you all that to me?!" he asked.

"Maybe you misjudged me," I said.

"I thought my feelings wouldn't deceive me, so I didn't even consider the idea of you rejecting me."

"What made you think that no one could ever reject you?!"

"I don't know if what I'm saying now is right or wrong, but I believe that inside each of us, no matter how humble we are, there is a voice that says you are special, you can paint pictures, you can play symphonies, you can do anything you set your mind to, you can do everything and anything, because inside you, deep down, you have extraordinary abilities. You are too special to be rejected. As they say, when God gave people their sustenance, no one was satisfied with their lot, but when He gave people minds, everyone was satisfied with their own. everyone sees themselves as the smartest of the smart and their opinion as the most correct at all times and on all subjects. However, I know that many are smarter than me, many are more handsome than me, and many are better than me in morals, knowledge, money, talents, and everything else," he said.

"But I loved you and did not consider the possibility of rejection, so I went into a great battle without a plan for retreat, which caused total destruction of the heart with a disorganised, defeated retreat, dripping with pieces and blood from the bloody wound that remains open to this day. Heart wounds take a very long time to heal, unlike physical wounds, which heal and fade quickly, leaving no trace, unlike heart wounds, which may never heal," he continued.

"What makes you so special that you cannot be rejected?" I asked.

"I am special because I love you, I love you truly and sincerely. I am special because I am yours and you are mine, because I belong to you and you belong to me. I would shower you with all the beautiful words in the world. I would delve deep into the study of our language to search for new meanings, and I would spend hours writing poems and verses for you. I would also study every language I could get my hands on so that I could tell you I love you in a thousand ways. I would fulfil your wishes before you even said them, before you even opened your lips, before the thought even flashed in your eyes, before the idea even crossed your mind. I will be silent with you, gazing into your eyes on the banks of the rivers for hours at sunset, and at night, we will gaze at the moon together. We will dance to soft music all night long. We will go out on the weekend to eat out, go to the cinema, have fun in a park, and visit places. I will protect you; I will take care of you, I will give you all your rights and I will not restrict you; I will let you be yourself, and I will not put you in a mould that I have created in my mind from my own ideas and thoughts," he said.

"Your feelings might come out of hundreds of men, but you never bothered to see me and tell what I really want and need. Why didn't you forget me immediately and mature like many young people do?" I asked.

"I spent a whole year loving you in silence without telling you what was in my heart, without even seeing you. Then I spent half a year trying unsuccessfully to get close to you, sometimes hinting at my admiration for you, then, in involuntary shyness, I would drop hints to the contrary, telling you that you were not on my mind. When we had the opportunity to talk alone, I would retreat and run away in fear and embarrassment. When I picked up the phone to call you, it would remain in my hand for more than half an hour, I would pace back and forth across the room, and after dialling your number ten times, I would hang up before completing the seven digits. I would put down the phone and go about my business. Whenever I found the courage to speak to you, I would talk in generalities, stammering and afraid. and I don't say 90% of what I intended to say to you. So, I talk to you in my mind with the most beautiful and eloquent words all week long, and when I meet you, my tongue ties and I can't say a word of what I said to you in my mind. Instead, I say things I didn't want to say to you, and then I see you looking at me with contempt, and then you walk away," he said.

It seemed like, he had a lot trapped in his heart and mind for so long; so, I kept silent, as he continued:

"On many long nights, I dreamt of you in many forms and ways. Sometimes I only saw you smiling, other times you talked to me at length about something, and other times you showered me with overflowing feelings of love and tenderness, making me the happiest and luckiest man in the world, until I woke up and everything disappeared, leaving only a confused tear, a question mark, and a faint smile tainted by sadness. In many dreams, I eloquently confess my love for you, sometimes on the bus, sometimes in the park, sometimes on the street, and sometimes in front of the house of worship where I first met you," he said.

I knew my main role here is to listen; so I did as he continued:

"And so, you filled my waking hours and my sleep, even after the little dream came true and I confessed my love for you. Now you wake me up from that dream with force, after I built my whole life around you, you tore yourself away from my being, and when you took away my foundation, you left me to collapse and fall... You know, for a moment I told myself that she might reject me, and when that thought came to me, I said to her: So be it, even if she rejects me, it is enough for me to let her know that one day someone loved her with all this love. The truth is that I am still stunned, and I have come to you to answer a question that is burning in my mind: Why did you reject me?"

"In my mind, you are not the man of my dreams. You are too kind for my liking. With my calmness, simplicity and kindness, I don't want these qualities in my husband. I want him to be mischievous, to speak eloquently with everyone, both boys and girls, to wear the finest clothes and the most beautiful perfumes. He has a pride that provokes people to try their hardest to please him, even though he is empty, so stingy with his smiles that some people make it their life's goal to make him smile. He treats people harshly and rudely, because that's how life is, and..."

"Enough, enough, enough! You are talking about a person who is far from me, a person I don't even enjoy dealing with," he interrupted me.

"Do you understand me now?" I asked.

"Yes, I only understand you now. I was wrong in my judgement of you. I loved someone other than you in my imagination. Only now do I understand that the mistake was not mine, or yours, but in the image I created of you on my own for so long, in the lack of understanding and communication between us, and in my surrender to emotions that deceive and distort the image for their own sake. Now I thank you for making me understand this truth, and I thank you for your time and wish you success in your life. And now, goodbye?"

"Goodbye," I said with a smile, then left, amazed by that strange day.

15

Today is the day we've been waiting for, the day we've been longing for. The time has come, and I will know if the malicious trick I played has worked.

Months ago, I began writing letters to a diverse group of people of different ages, religions, orientations, and cultures. I did not know any of them personally. My goal was to conduct a study on anxiety, dreams, illusions, realities, and the extent to which all of these affect human behaviour.

This was the title of my letter: "A Letter from a Higher Power." The text of my letter was as follows:

To Mr. So-and-so, son of So-and-so, son of Noah, son of Adam,

It has been decided that you will move to us and join our ranks at such-and-such a time on such-and-such a day of such-and-such a month of such-and-such a year in such-and-such a manner.

Do not take our message lightly, for you are not the first with whom we have done this. What do you have to lose by being cautious? Think of it as a warning message to end your commitments on this earth, your unfinished and pending affairs, and your unstable relationships before you leave this world.

Think of it as a message telling you that your mobile phone credit has run out and that you will not be able to make any more calls until you top up your card. It is a new system that we are now using to see how useful it is and what effect it has on people, and to see whether it is worthwhile for a person to know the date of their death well in advance or not. Can a person change from one extreme to the other and improve their life in a few months? You are one of the lucky ones we have chosen to apply this offer to, so please do not waste the opportunity by doubting it and take these words seriously for your worldly and eternal benefit!

See you forever, together, at the appointed time.

A higher heavenly authority.

...

And so ends my letter.

I am not the first to have had this strange idea. Someone else did it once, showering their victim with messages saying that they would die at a time specified to the second, minute, hour, day, month, and year, in a manner specified in minute detail. The letters were signed with a message from the other world, and with the abundance of letters, the poor victim had no choice but to involuntarily unconsciously think about the content of those poisonous words.

As a result of their subconscious mind storing these words, the victim lived in constant anxiety, turning into a ticking time bomb waiting to explode. The closer the appointed time came, the more anxiety, depression, fits of rage, rebellion, sadness, fear, trembling, and uprising increased in the poor victim's soul. Their heart protested against the fear and pain it had endured by stopping its contractions to pump blood, even before the date specified in the letter.

If that victim were to live until the date specified in the letter, she would meet her death by cardiac arrest, at exactly the appointed time, after the subconscious mind gave the conscious mind the impression that the victim had died. The poor entity – I mean the subconscious mind – is convinced of this fact, and the conscious mind stands stunned by this surprise and gives orders to the body to destroy the latter. The body cannot live without the mind, whether it is the conscious mind responsible for all the voluntary actions that a person performs, or the subconscious mind responsible for all the involuntary movements that the body performs without direct control from the person, such as the mechanics of breathing, bowel movements, and heartbeats.

The password here is belief. To be more accurate, the key principle is the power of belief, combined with the naivety of the conscious mind that let the belief pass inside the person, for the law of attraction of the subconscious mind to finish the job.

Now you can imagine the system that was put in place to eliminate that poor victim. First: the conscious mind was convinced that the victim would die on a specific date. Second: the conscious mind polluted the subconscious mind, even though the former rejected that discourse and rejected it wholeheartedly. Third: the conscious mind could not bear the terrible psychological pressure placed upon it, so it begged the subconscious mind to end its torment and relieve it of its pain. The subconscious mind responded and stopped one of the involuntary processes we mentioned earlier, or the conscious mind held on, patiently waiting until the appointed time, without begging the subconscious mind, so that the victim could survive that round.

Fourth and finally: When the victim approaches the appointed time, or reaches it, the subconscious mind realises that the time has come or is near, and does not respond to this with any pain, hesitation or sadness, for it has grown weary of that life with its fatigue. Do not forget that you sleep, but it does not; rather, it dreams and imagines. There is no sleep without dreams. Rather, when you say, "I had a dream," it is only on that day that you remember the dream. On all other days, you dream at night, but you do not remember the dream when you wake up, even at those times when you wander aimlessly without thinking, it is at work. Likewise, the subconscious mind is tired of all the involuntary commands it has issued throughout life.

In any case, the poor soul realises that their time has come, so the victim closes the curtain on the play of life on earth and issues a secret, silent, decisive, swift and effective order to the heart, saying one word: Enough. The heart stops as a result of that direct order, and the victim's life ends.

Today is the appointed day for the last person on my list, and when I see his fate, I will be able to write the data and realistic practical statistics for the case under study in my master's thesis, which specialises in inner psychology and its impact on external human behaviour. Of course, I have finished all the paperwork, and all that remains is to support my theories with practical experiments, which I will finish today.

Some people say I'm crazy. I don't know what you think about that, but I haven't found any other way to prove my hypotheses and my findings about the unique nature of the human psyche and body and the extent to which each part—the psyche and the body—affects the other, and the unusual relationship between the conscious mind and the subconscious mind, and the unique connection between the mind and the body.

As for my expectations for this last case, they are negative. I do not expect him to survive. What distinguishes him from the previous cases? Case number five committed suicide well before the appointed time, case number seven killed herself on the same day she was supposed to die, as specified in the letter, case number one suffered a heart attack, case number three stopped breathing after a sudden crisis that came without warning, case number nine died exactly on the appointed date without any specific reason, case number two went to sleep on the night before the date specified in the letter and did not wake up, there is the case that was completely paralysed, and the case that is now undergoing psychological treatment, which has been diagnosed as a rare and dangerous condition.

None of my cases survived. Only one man survived, just one man, but he was left in a state of permanent shock and chronic depression. You can tell this from his constant silence, his staring, bewildered eyes, and his sad, frozen features.

And so, all that remains is this case, which will end today, and tomorrow I will be able to finish my thesis, conclude, and rest. All I have to do today is watch closely and take notes. Here I am, riding in a hired car, following him in the taxi he got into hours ago and has not yet left. What are all these visits that clumsy man is making? The important thing is to follow him until the end of the day to see the final result.

Hush! Don't make a sound in the seat next to the driver, lest he notice us and all my efforts be wasted. Wait with me in silence and calm.

...

...

...

16

"Hello," she said, answering the phone.

"Hello," he replied.

"Is (Peep, peep, car horns) there, Auntie?"

"No, he's not there. Shall we tell him who wants him when he gets back?"

"But when will he be back?"

"We don't know when he'll be back, he didn't say, he's at his uncle's. If you need him urgently, call him there. Do you want the phone number?"

"Yes, please. Give it to me."

"It's .... (You're doing this to me, you son of a b****, street fight)."

"Thank you."

"You're welcome."

"Goodbye."

"Goodbye."

• • •

"Hello," his uncle said, answering the phone

"Hello," same man replied.

"Is .... (Peep, car horn) there, please?"

"He's in the bathroom."

"Never mind, I'll call him back in half an hour."

"He is."

"Goodbye."

"Goodbye."

• • •

"Hello."

"Hello."

"May I speak to .... (Neighbours fighting, domestic fight), please?"

"Hold on a second."

"Hello."

"How are you, man?"

"I'm fine, thank God. But who is this?"

"It's me."

"Hey! Wow! You're calling me after all these years. Wow! How did you remember me after all this time?!"

"It's a revival of time and memories, mate."

"Wow! How are things with you?"

"Good. Listen!"

"What?!"

"I wanted to tell you something."

"What is it?!"

"We didn't talk much, and we didn't know each other very well, but I wanted to tell you that I always respected you and liked you for your good looks, your elegance, your hard work, your good character, and your kindness to others, but I never told you any of this because I was embarrassed and shy to say it."

"Thank you, my friend. I also liked you. Although our conversations were short and few, they were deep, honest, and direct, worth a thousand sentences and a million words. I was truly happy to know you, and even when life forces us to be busy all the time with our work, our families, and our activities, we will never forget those people who influenced us, affected us, and whom we affected. They live within us with their thoughts and dreams, breathe with our hearts, and do everything they used to do when we lived with them."

"Well done, my friend."

"So, my image will always be with you!"

"I hope I have an image inside you too!"

"It's there, my friend. Believe me!"

"I believe you, my friend, and thank you."

"No thanks among friends? Don't say that!"

"Where are you working now?"

"........ And you?"

"........ And how are things with you?"

"Fine, the usual happens every day without any change, you know."

"Yes, I wish you well, my friend."

"You too."

"Goodbye."

"Goodbye."

17

There are owls, there are piercing glances from the eyes of men in ragged clothes, who are used to not seeing any life in their neighbourhood, there is an unpleasant, musty smell, there is a deadly silence like the silence of the dead, no, it is the silence of the dead because I am indeed in the cemetery. I do not know what prompted me to visit my father at this late hour, for the night, with the graveyard, with the dead, with the silence, created a frightening symphony that shake limbs, loosen joints, and terrify even the bravest of hearts. I pushed all those thoughts out of my mind and headed to my father's grave.

"Oh, Dad! How I miss you! How barren and desolate life seems without you! My only consolation is that you can hear me now, and that we will meet again. I am certain of this. Life is a test, Dad, in which you are tested on what you have learned from the book, and you answer before the committee with your deeds, your faith, your actions, and your thoughts, and then the paper is taken from you, but the problem is that you do not know when that paper will be taken. I hope you have passed, so that I may see you again. Oh Lord, save him and have mercy on him."

And he burst into a wave of hot tears. No, he didn't notice me or even realise I was there. I saw him as I was going to my father's grave, so I stopped to listen to what he was saying. I was extremely surprised to find someone else in the cemetery at that time of night, but it seems I'm not the only crazy person here. The strange thing is that the frightening atmosphere doesn't seem to affect that boy in the slightest.

The boy's voice became clear again after he finished his prayer:

"Do you remember, Dad, that day we argued and I made you angry? I'm sorry, I didn't mean to. I was just stressed at the time. I'm also sorry for all the things we disagreed on.

The room rules, driving, the shop, whatever... And... And... I really liked that sandwich you made that day... Thank you for helping me study throughout primary school. You never denied me anything."

I saw a bouquet of white roses, a wreath, and some small items on the boy's father's grave, and before I could hear any more, I left for my father's grave. I had left the house at that time to come here and ask my father if he approved of my marriage, but after what I had just heard, I didn't know what to say. So I stood in front of the grave, silent, confused and surprised. What could I say to a man who was no longer in this world? I racked my brain to come up with something appropriate to say, and...

"How are you, Father?!" I asked.

"...."

"I hope you are well," I said.

"...."

"I don't know if now is a good time, so I will come by tomorrow. There is something important I would like to consult with you about. I will prepare tea in the thermos, and we can drink it together as we usually do when we discuss important matters," I said.

A tear fell from my eye, and I hurried outside.

∞

I will die today at any moment.

I learned this from a letter. At first, I did not pay any attention to it and did not believe a single word it contained, but as the days passed, I found that the fear of death was taking over every fibre of my being. It is true that death comes without warning, so what is to prevent it from coming before the date specified in the letter? So, the idea of not being prepared for death terrified me, prompting me to try to improve my life to be better than it is now.

I began to ask myself what I do during my day and how I spend my time. I started to eliminate everything I used to do that was useless, until I knew exactly what I should do in my life on earth as a place of waiting. Then I began to do it, to the point that I began to long for death so that I could meet my Lord, my God, and my Creator.

So I woke up at six, prayed, ate my breakfast, left my house, met that child at 1, went to the post office where I made an agreement with that man at 2, and then I had to save every second of my precious time; I felt the value of time so strongly that I made an agreement with the taxi driver at 3.

The taxi took me to my first destination, the house of worship, where I prayed at 4. On the way, I stopped at the toy shop at 5, and from there I went to the hospital to visit a sick friend early before visiting hours ended at 6. Then I went to meet the girl I had loved since I was six years old at 7.

Then, in the taxi, I wrote a letter to the supervisor of my thesis and gave it to the lab assistant on my fifth taxi ride to the college at 8. Before leaving the college, I went to that lecture where I met a dear friend whom I had not seen for many months, I do not know how many, at 9, and then to the workplace of another married friend who needed money from me earlier. I went on the sixth taxi ride at 10.

Then I felt hungry, so I went to the kushari restaurant at 11, and from there to a telephone booth, where I made a series of calls that resulted in contacting my soldier friend's unit at 12. Then I visited a friend at his home to teach him the tricks of the trade and the secrets of the profession at 13. After that, I met my beloved, whom I had loved for two years in silence without confessing my love to her, at 14.

At 16, I went to the nearest telephone booth to call a dear colleague whom I had not forgotten for years, then I went to visit my father in the cemetery at 17.

When evening came, I returned home. As for me, I never knew the content of 15, but now you know it, and you can also know that I did not die in fear and terror, but rather that the heavy joke that happened to me taught me how to live life in the right way. I did not exist in that life by chance, but rather God created me for a purpose. and I must live, breathe, and act in the world to please my Creator.

The three hands raced to the number 12 on the clock, and at 11 o'clock, the hour hand began its slow journey, and the minute hand began its long journey. The last minutes passed as I prayed fervently. When there was one minute left until midnight, and both the hour and minute hands had one last tick left, the second hand ran eagerly, gnawing at the clock face, until the three hands met at the same point, and... time stopped at that point...

And...

I did not die, I did not die. Of course, I knew that the letter was a joke, and when I did not die, I did not know the purpose of that letter, but it really benefited me. Now that I know the truly important things in life, I will not waste time again. I will spend my time wisely and not waste it. I will go to meet the love of my life at 7, and I will live as I should live. I will live every day of my life as if it were my last, and every moment as if it were my last.

Do you understand now what you have read? You have been reading the story of a dying man, eating his last meal, praying his last prayer, making amends with people, doing what he wished he could do all his life in one day, and rebuilding broken bridges with others.

You now know that my story was narrated by seventeen characters, and that I was the one who did everything that happened in those chapters. Of course, after learning that all the events in the story took place in a single day, you now understand the meaning of the title. 1440. It is the number of minutes in a day, the number you get when you multiply the number of hours in a day by the number of minutes in an hour.

• • •

Cairo, November 2005

NOVEL II
WOMAN

We are all worthy and deserving of love and happiness.
To all who suffered abuse, neglect and rejection,
may you find peace and joy.

Reality
Narrated By The Man

1- THE JOURNEY

This man undertook this journey to earn more money, as his salary was not enough to cover his expenses. This young man intends to propose to his girlfriend as soon as he returns from his journey, and he is now thinking about how to propose, where, when, and how he will tell her. That little girl is grieving over the loss of the toy she loved. That boy is thinking about how to defeat his arch-rival and competitor at work. That man who has finished his years of work and is now retired is standing in secret prayer, but you do not know that. That unemployed young man is planning to win over that girl who stands far away, but you don't know about his plan. That boy went on that trip for work. That girl went on that trip for tourism. That man and that woman are spending their honeymoon. Those two men went on that trip to carry out a scam.

I was the boy who went on that trip for work, and I was also the one who observed the other passengers on the ship that took us to that distant country and deduced their motives for travelling.

Sitting on that seat in front of that table among these people, I looked at my cup of coffee sleepily and let my mind wander into nothingness.

It was one of those comfortable moments when your mind oscillates between consciousness and unconsciousness. You are not fully conscious of life, nor are you asleep and unconscious, nor are you dead and absent from your body, nor are you drunk and confused. You are in that moment of restlessness when all sounds fall silent.

I contemplated the smoke rising from the surface of the dark brown coffee and wondered in silence where my years had gone and how I had spent my days. When the smoke disappeared and the hot coffee turned into warm coffee, I knew where they had gone. I held the cup in my fingers, caressed it with my thumb, brought it close to my mouth, and before it even touched my lips, I exhaled violently, scattering the coffee. I tried in vain to drink what remained of the surface of the coffee, as if the surface of the coffee were different from what lay beneath it. I drank the brown liquid with relish, and when I finished and looked at the empty cup, I wondered where the smoke had gone, where the surface of the coffee had disappeared, and where the coffee itself had vanished! Perhaps the smoke was meant to evaporate into the air, the surface to be scattered by the wind, and the coffee to be absorbed by my stomach.

What am I thinking?! Didn't I tell you that I am in that stage between consciousness and unconsciousness?! I warned you, but you insist on sitting with me.

I rested my left hand on my bag, which was lying on the seat next to me, as if I were shaking hands with an old friend, enjoying the company on that journey. Oh, my clothes! Although you have been attached to me all my life, you have never felt me! Did my primary school clothes feel my confusion? Did my military jacket feel my loneliness? Or perhaps my lab coat felt my thoughts and ambitions? They are clothes, just clothes, a cheap cover for the precious body, the human body that in turn covers the soul. I have always cared more about what is inside me than what is outside, and my main concern has been to purify and improve my inner self rather than care about my appearance. However, people often only look at what is outside and are usually unable to see what is inside.

The waiter came, placed the coffee cup on a tray, and looked at me politely, asking with a glance that could convey many meanings: Are you not leaving? Where is the bill? Is there anything else? Have you lost your voice? At the same time, I was thinking I don't know if I want to leave or not, and if I want to leave, I don't know where to go, and if I go there, I don't know what I will do. As the saying goes: If you don't know where you're going, all roads lead there. The process of thinking itself seemed unprecedentedly exhausting. It occurred to me that I needed an active mind to think with, and a fresh cup of coffee would be an excellent choice.

"Could I have another cup of coffee with extra sugar?"

He replied politely:

"Of course, sir."

Where did the word 'sir' come from? What is its connection to the army? These are all questions I don't know the answers to, and to be honest, I don't care to know. What good would my knowledge do me other than to show off in front of others, so they feel ignorant and inferior to me, and hate me for no reason other than feeling weak in my presence? I definitely don't want to know, I just want my coffee.

I looked at my key ring lying on the table and remembered. That friend gave it to me, or should I say that enemy? There is no mystery about it. He was my friend and I was his enemy. It's as simple as that.

2- THE FRIEND

We were children in the third grade, that age when we begin to exist, to feel our selfhood and being in some way, when we are controlled by our feelings and temperament without the restraint of reason or willpower. That friend beat me up for a reason I did not know at the time, as I was too young to analyse people's personalities and deduce their motives. Now I know that he was jealous of me, perhaps because I was loved by my classmates and teachers, or perhaps because I was diligent and hard-working, or for some other reason that hardly matters.

The funny thing is that those who appear strong in that life are in fact weak, because they are driven by their animal instincts and their fleeting emotions. A person only needs someone who loves them as they are, cares for them, makes them feel present and important. Because I somehow realised these truths, I did not abuse him, hit him or mistreat him. Instead, I loved him with pure love, without the slightest feeling of hatred and without pretence. I longed to see him, listened to his every word with interest, and sought opportunities to serve him or express my concern, whether with important information or with a sandwich of luncheon meat that we used to breastfeed after milk in our primary schools.

I felt deep down that I was doing the right thing, because if I had done otherwise and hit him, he would have brought his friends to confront me, and I would have brought others, and the issue would have escalated, causing endless problems. He would have plotted against me, and I would plan another one for him, and the cycle of revenge would only end with forgiveness or bloodshed, and if not with spilled blood, then with blood stained in veins with resentment. I did not want to cloud my thinking with those negative feelings and that pent-up anger, and with the tension and anxiety that would accompany thoughts of tit-for-tat and revenge.

And I was right, because a person who harbours negative feelings can change their direction to become positive feelings, which is better than a person who has no feelings to give to another. We then became best friends, and our relationship continued from primary school through to university.

My mother instilled in me feelings of love for all people, and she always taught me that if I hated one person among a million, my heart would be clouded with darkness that would soon contaminate it completely. Therefore, I must love all people, serve them, and give them my full energy without expecting anything in return. I should not even wait for the look of happiness on their faces. I should not change my character according to other people's character but should remain true to myself. I should not change my material; I should remain gold even when surrounded by tin. I should give even if the other party stops giving.

I looked around and thought, regardless of our races on that ship, our genders, our ethnicities, and our beliefs, I felt that we were all one fabric of different shapes and colours, for in the end, we are all one creation. We were all inside our father Adam one day, we were cells in his body in a way, philosophers agree on that, there is (Yung) who spoke about the collective unconscious and how heritage affects individual behaviour, clergymen also agree on the idea of one body of which we humans are members.

If a citizen of India is in pain, I must be affected in some way. We are connected in some way, one fabric, one entity, so we must love ourselves and love others, forgive ourselves and forgive others, and respect ourselves and respect others.

That friend emigrated to that distant country, where he has been working and living for years.

It settled there in the medal in that ethereal place, this key, the key to our apartment where my mother lives, and the details of my birth, as I later learned, came to mind when he placed the cup of coffee on the table next to the medal.

3- A BOY IS BORN

The nurses rushed down the wide corridor of that modest hospital, which indicated their lack of competence and the seriousness of the condition of the woman giving birth to her fifth child.

The father puffed on his cigarette in anger, weariness and sadness. His wife had already given birth to four daughters, and he was now waiting for the fifth, hoping it would be a boy.

Here he was, arguing with his mother-in-law:

"God is my witness, if she gives me another girl, I will slaughter her and the newborn together," he said.

His mother-in-law patted him on the shoulder to calm him down, knowing that it was too early to try to reach a compromise. Why should she jump the gun and convince him that a girl is just as good as a boy and that whatever God decrees is good, when her daughter had not yet given birth? She had told him this scenario three times before, and she refused to repeat herself a fourth time. She could only mutter one word:

"Be patient!"

The father felt angry at himself for what he had said, and his eyes filled with tears, not out of concern for his poor wife, who was facing death while giving birth to his fifth child, but out of regret and anger at himself.

"I'm sorry, mother," he said in anger.

"Forgive me, mother. Of course I am concerned for the safety of your daughter, for she is my beloved wife. However, you must understand that the costs and expenses of life are greater than I can bear. We barely have enough to live on, and I cannot bear to have another daughter in the family without a son. I know that I am childish in my thinking, and I know that I will not bequeath him much money. In fact, he will be lucky if he does not inherit debts. I will not honour him with a name he will be proud of forever, but I will give him a very ordinary name, like all the other names. I will not deliver him to a beautiful, friendly world that will greet him with hugs, smiles and warmth. Rather, I will bring him into a harsh world where he will struggle his whole life to secure a place for himself that he will soon leave to others. But I want him. I want my son. I have been dreaming of him since my youth," he said.

And there, in front of those buried feelings, the man cried, and the woman cried, moved by his emotion and fear for her daughter's labour pains, and for that unstable, anxious, angry husband.

"Everything will be fine," she said.

She prayed from the bottom of her heart that her daughter's womb would produce a boy, so that God would protect her from the blows of fate and the evil of her husband. Only her husband was not evil, but faced the situation like a child, not a man. He had been raised in such a pampered manner that he grew up to be a big child rather than a man. When he married, his wife became his mother, and she played that role well, being a mother to everyone: her husband, her family, the residents of her house, and all people. She was affectionate and generous, and a mother is a symbol of tenderness, love, sacrifice, and generosity.

Of course, the husband did not mean what he said about killing her and the baby. He was speaking with the mind and feelings of a child placed in the position of a man and given the authority of an Eastern husband. Therefore, it is not fair to hold him accountable for what he said and to consider his words as mere childish talk. We should love him as a man, be kind to him as a child, and rely on him as a human being. He is both a father and a son to his son at the same time, which is a strange and incomprehensible paradox. His pampering makes him seek praise and appreciation from everyone he meets, even if it is his young son whose father should be showering him with praise.

Only those who realise these truths will give that man the pampering he wants and the appreciation he seeks, and will not compete with him for attention, and will live happily with him for the rest of their lives. My mother was the one who realised these truths.

And I came. This is when it all began.

Complete darkness, complete silence, complete rest.

So I remained in that darkness for nine months without having to move a single muscle in my body. I did not need to breathe, chew, digest, or even swallow my saliva, as air, food, and drink came to me directly from my mother.

I will never forget the moment I came into the world. I couldn't open my eyes because of the intense light, and my body was overcome by extreme cold as the dust-laden air entered my lungs. It was more than I could bear. How cruel life is!

And so I let out a heart-wrenching cry. I don't think I will ever forget that painful experience as long as I live, or at least the memory of it will remain in my heart. The need to return to a place of comfort and safety.

Then I drank the liquid of life, breast milk. I had to choose between the painful process of swallowing and starving to death, and I chose to swallow. Over time, I mastered it.

Of course, everyone was happy with my arrival. My mother was happy because she had made my father happy, and my father was happy because he had got what he wanted. Even my sisters were happier after my father calmed down towards them and became gentler and kinder after he got what he wanted. Of course, I was the cause of their jealousy, but they felt at ease after I arrived. You make others feel at ease if you are at ease, and you upset them if you are upset. Feelings are contagious, my friend, so do not blame those who frown at you if you frown at them first.

4- THE PRINCIPLES OF LIFE

And so my mother fed me food for the soul after feeding me food for the body, and she kept repeating those words to me.

Love and be kind to everyone around you. When you care for another person with genuine concern that comes from within your heart, you are giving them the most beautiful thing you can give. Do not focus on yourself but open up to people. Do not drown in the abyss of your own existence. Help and serve people, to find a way out of the selfishness that empty people fall into. Your goal is to make people happy, for only then will you feel happy yourself. You will not be happy if you try to seek happiness for yourself on your own. We were created as a group, not as individuals, so we get to know that there is no point in being alone. We have reproduced until we have come to know that we are all connected in some way.

Then I contemplated the key that follows the key to our flat. It is the key to our new home, which we bought after the building that housed our first flat collapsed in the earthquake that shook the country many years ago. I remember that day well.

My grandmother was ill and wanted to see us, so my sisters and I went with my mother to my grandmother's house, while my father, exhausted after a long day, told us he was going to sleep to regain his energy. So we left him and went out, only for him to meet his death that day under the rubble, leaving us wondering what might have been.

What if he hadn't been lazy and had come with us? What if we hadn't gone and had woken him up in time to get everyone out of the house before it collapsed? What if my grandmother hadn't fallen ill and we had all stayed at home that day to meet our silent fate? What if my father hadn't been exhausted from work, even if the amount of work he had to do that day had been reduced? What if the agency that works with the company that deals with the office that my father's institution deals with hadn't dumped all that work on my father that day? What if my father's love for his mother-in-law had been greater than his exhaustion from work?

A thousand questions and one answer: what happened has happened and cannot be changed. God's perfect justice is beyond doubt, and what happened is for the best and was planned by the Controller of all things. It is for the good of all those who love God. Gratitude is tested by crises and complaining and grumbling are signs of a lack of faith. And so we submitted to God's will and thanked Him for what we will understand tomorrow—even if it is after our death—that it is good for everyone.

Last year, my last sister got married, leaving only my mother and me in the house. They are all married now and each of them is happy in her husband's home. I married them all off, covered their expenses, invested everything I had in their marriages, and borrowed money for years to come. I say I invested, not wasted, because I consider my life an investment in what I do for others. What if I hadn't been existed? What would the lives of others have been like? Life would certainly have gone on without me, but I am happy that I pushed the wheel of life forward and helped others. I would not have been happy if I had not done what I did, and I am completely satisfied and pleased with what I did. If I could turn back time, I would live the same life again.

Time has passed and so be it. It will pass anyway, and in any case, it will not stop for any creature or linger over any human being. The giant wheel of fate will continue to turn at its steady pace, constantly moving to crush beneath it all those who dare to rebel and rage against the laws of the universe and the nature of creation.

Let time pass.

5- THE MEDAL

The key that follows the key to the new house is the key to the office.

I work. A man does not only work to earn his daily bread and meet his personal needs, but also to feel his existence and himself, to benefit society with what he does, and to push the wheel of human development forward. However, society did not allow me the luxury of choosing the job that suits me and that I love.

Instead, I was presented with a job opportunity, so I took it, as it was not easy to find a job in that crowded country that was tight for you to even breath. Because job opportunities were few and far between in our beloved country, I had to seize it and look for another opportunity while working in the one available.

However, life did not allow me the time to look for another opportunity, as I spent most of my time at work fulfilling my sisters' requests. Thus, I got used to loving my job. My job was not the job I had hoped for, but it was just a job. However, I forced myself to love it in order to perform well, and I did. I loved those in it, and they loved me. When all doors were closed to me, I found my work to be an open door that I could enter at any time to distract me from all the thoughts and concerns of the world. Then the economic crisis that shook the entire world occurred, and they told me frankly that I had to resign before they dismissed me in their own way, and I did.

It is another test of patience, another test of gratitude. I must not get angry, or revolt, or curse, only give thanks. Surely there is good behind all this, only my limitations prevent me from seeing the good behind events. I will be patient.

Speaking of patience, there was that tiny key in the medallion. It is the key to the savings box that my schoolmate gave me. My schoolmate is the girl who loved me with all her heart and soul, who would light up her fingers for me, and whose greatest hope was to see me happy. Of course, I loved her like a sister, and because she was my friend, the feelings of affection between us grew, and because she was a girl, the feelings of friendship between us grew even stronger.

She knows that I cannot afford the costs of marriage, and she knows that I treat her like a sister, but she loved me with great intensity and strength. There is no force that can stand in the way of a woman when she loves and when she realises and is certain that she loves. Women are mostly indecisive, hesitant and confused. The nature of a hesitant woman makes her suspicious of everything all the time and makes her imagine that there is always a plot being hatched behind her back. Her imagination influences her decisions, so she imagines things and interprets actions based on assumptions she has made from words she has not heard but only imagines hearing.

When a woman is certain of something, nothing can dissuade her, even if the whole world shouts at her and casts doubt on what she has concluded. That woman loved me and was certain of her feelings towards me, and there was no turning back. The bullet had left the barrel, the milk had been spilt, the match had been struck, and there was no going back.

How cruel it is to be rejected by someone who loves you. It is crueller than being rejected yourself.

When someone else rejects you, your mind will return you to your natural state, and you will console yourself. Even if your feelings are squeezed out, you alone will suffer for a limited time until the giant foot of oblivion steps on you and crushes your memories into particles invisible to the naked eye, disappearing into the corners of your spherical heart.

You will tell yourself that life is full of many things, she rejected me, and others may reject me too. I am not so special that I cannot be rejected, and even if I were very special, not all girls would like me. You will tell yourself that she is very special, and I am also special. She is a red pearl, and I am a blue diamond. We are both special, and we are both good, but we are just not right for each other, and that does not make either of us flawed. You will control your feelings with your mind, and you will occupy your time with many things and forget her.

However, you will be helpless when you realise that with your tongue you will hurt the feelings of a person whose only sin in life was to love you, give you everything she had, entrust you with everything she owns, and give you everything she will ever have. All you will be able to do is make excuses to distance yourself from her without hurting her feelings, but that is impossible, for she will not accept any substitute for you, no matter what.

"I'm not suited for marriage, and by then you'll be too old," I told her. "I'll wait for you no matter how long it takes," she replied. "You'll surely find someone better than me," I said. "Even if I do, I won't accept him as my lover," she insisted. "I have nothing," I told her, so she bought this savings box and gave me the key and said she was satisfied and content with every penny I put in it, even if it was only one penny. I told her to look for someone else, and she told me she saw no one but me. I told her I was a wreck of a man, and she assured me that she would make me fit for residence. I told her my heart was dry of feelings, and she told me she was the stream that God had written for me.

She is the woman who loves. If my rejection offends her dignity, it may be the end. She may despise me and love me at the same time. I would not be able to predict her actions then, nor would she. Her actions would stem from the great love in her heart and the deep wound to her pride, producing random feelings of anger and tenderness, love and disgust, violence and submissiveness, harshness and gentleness.

Thank God I have not hurt her dignity so far, and I have not acted in this regard yet. I got a job opportunity in that distant country after leaving my job, and she knew that I had no choice but to travel, and no other option available after all those debts piled up on my shoulders.

My mind tells me to end her pain so that she can continue her life with someone else who deserves her love and affection, but my heart refuses to hurt the one I love so much. I am tormented by the terrible pain of causing all this confusion and pain to a woman who loved me so much, but I have no choice. I cannot take her as my lover against my will. I will make myself miserable by doing so, and with time she will sense my rejection of her, and all the love in her heart will turn to contempt after I fail to reciprocate her feelings, and I will become a source of humiliation to her femininity after rejecting her, even if unconsciously. Women feel, and with the pain squeezing my heart, there is a hidden happiness that comes from the fact that one of them loved me so much. I began to pity myself for my inability to reciprocate her feelings, and I praised myself for making that decision, which shows intellectual maturity to a large extent.

What a terrible circle of contradictions I had fallen into, and I still hadn't gotten out of it. The confused girl is still waiting for me till now.

I looked at the new cup of coffee. It had lost its heat, its steam had evaporated, and its surface had disappeared for no reason. and its liquid had lost the warmth of life and existence, becoming like a lifeless body with no soul inhabiting it. I had to pour it down the drain instead of into my stomach, as it was no longer of any use. I imagined that if I wasted my time in life like this, I would end up like that cup, thrown into the sink without anyone drinking me. What an end!

Despite my aversion to drinking hot beverages cold, I drank the contents of the cup in one gulp, feeling sorry for it, paid the waiter his fee, and went up to the deck, longing for more fresh air, as if the air where I was, was somehow polluted with my thoughts and ruminations, and that if I wanted to change those thoughts, I had to change the place where they came from in my mind.

6- THE AIR

And so I stood contemplating nature, gazing at the dark waters with fear and apprehension. I used to go out when I was sad and confused about life to that river that flows in our country. I would contemplate it at night, and the funny thing is that I would be sad before seeing it, then I would become even sadder after doing so. The gentle waves moving with the wind, the darkness, and the dim moonlight all cast incomprehensible and unanalysable emotions into the soul, feelings of the approaching hour, if those dark waters were to swallow you up and restrain you in their highly viscous waters, stifling your breath after blocking the air to your nose, or with the unlimited depth of the waters and their surface that also extends without limits, with the insignificance and limitations of man, with the mystery shrouded in darkness that may contain anything.

But now, standing before that ocean, I had nothing but silence and awe, and my mind was completely silent, just as if the soul had a wine that made it absent from feeling, so I was lost from the world of feeling by contemplating the ocean.

The waves rose, the wind raged, and I did not care! The ship swayed and tilted on its sides. The situation was very dangerous. The sailors were running around, the workers were floundering, the men were trampling on each other, the women were screaming in terror, and I knew that there was nothing I could do and that the ship was sinking!

I don't know why King Lear came to mind, facing the storm in Shakespeare's play. Lear did not care about his life, like a warrior who does not fear his enemy because he no longer cares about life and no longer cares whether he survives or not. The two things were equal to him, but I was not afraid because of my complete trust in God's justice, mercy, and love.

And so I opened my chest to the water and the wind.

I remember the job I did not find myself in and was satisfied with, I remember my classmate who loved me whom I did not love, I remember my father whom I did not have enough of, I remember my mother -the most beautiful creature in the world- whom I left, I remember my sisters with their four husbands.

And the ship sank!

And with it, all plans sank. It did not choose who to destroy but took everyone with it. I found the waves throwing me, picking me up, slapping me, carrying me, invading me, and withdrawing from me. All this in complete randomness, and everything I did of my own free will seemed useless. I was like someone struggling for existence inside his mother's womb, not knowing that all his struggles would end in failure, and that he would come out at the appointed time.

The same thing, my death is a matter of time, so there is no need to fight. I saw the people around me being buried by the wind, swallowed by the water, and digested by the bottom. My arms, which had been resisting the waves, gave way, and I drowned. Once again, my mother's voice appeared deep inside me: "There is a reason for everything, no matter how bad it seems, you just don't understand."

And so my arms moved again and I kept swimming, swimming, swimming, resisting the waves. I opened my eyes with difficulty amid the spray of the waves and found no end to the water in any direction. Why and where was I swimming to? There was no answer, but the right thing to do was to swim. My limitations prevented me from seeing land, but somewhere in my mind, I knew I had to head east towards the sun, as that was our destination. If I was going to find anything, I would find it in that direction.

And so I swam and swam. The water swallowed everything: dreams of wealth, the love of loved ones, children's games, the hatred of rivals, the prayers of believers, the simplicity of the joyful, the melting of couples, the evil of hatred, and the dreams of youth. That piece of fabric moved from here to another place.

My muscles ached and hurt, but I continued and continued. I saw no one around me; they were either somewhere else or they had all drowned. I couldn't go on. I relaxed my body to rest a little, then continued swimming, occupying my mind so that fatigue would not cause me to lose consciousness or push me into sleep, which would be the end for me. I had to think about anything.

My mind was unable to recall any images: the waiter, the coffee, the café, the passengers, the ship, the house, work, my mother, my schoolmate, a new life, a new page. Life had closed all its doors in my country. It was a clear message for me to move on. I couldn't change my time, but I could change my place. When all doors close their shutters, it means I must leave my tears at their thresholds and knock on the abandoned door covered in untouched dust.

Was the new page the final page? So be it. I am grateful for the breaths I took on that land. Oh God, receive my soul. Perhaps this was the moment when I would get the answers to everything. Your justice does not mean that there is no retribution here on earth and above in heaven, only that retribution here on earth may be delayed, perhaps by years, decades or centuries, but justice prevails.

I relaxed, continued swimming, and kept moving my arms. It is stronger than me. It is not just my desire to live and exist that is enough to keep me alive. There are laws for this earth we live on, and there are limits to the capabilities of the human body that I am now using to live.

I do not know when my strength failed me, when my mind wandered, or when I lost consciousness. All I know is that all of this happened.

FANTASY
NARRATED BY FATE

7- THE BATTLE

A fiery beam of light flashed in the heart of the darkness and struck the man's chest like thunder. The Amazon saw the glint in his eyes in the darkness of the night, so she came out from behind the tree branch she was hiding behind and aimed her arrow at the man's heart. She released it, racing against time, cutting through the air to pierce the man's ribs.

The wind blowing to the left at that speed meant that she had to deflect her hand to the right by that amount. The light morning dew would weigh down the arrow in the air, which meant that she had to raise her hand by that amount. She held her breath, froze her muscles, and tightened her fingers around the tail of the arrow, then released it quickly and smoothly, spinning it between her fingers in a clockwise direction to give it a spinning effect in the air, maintaining its direction and increasing its speed.

This is how you see her, with flowing golden yellow hair, on her bare shiny shoulders, ending in two snow-white arms, and from there to two forearms adorned with two bracelets of pure gold, a golden breastplate studded with diamonds, followed by a bare stomach, ending with a second armoured piece covering the waist, From that piece emerge two pieces of silk, one in front and one in back, covering her down to her knees, shiny yellow silk from which bare legs emerge behind it, ending in pointed shoes with sharp golden yellow heels, though made of leather reinforced with metal.

A queen, the queen of the Amazons.

She had gone out early that morning with three warriors from her personal retinue when she saw a group of savage Berbers. She counted them with her eyes and found them to be about fifty, so she ordered the three warriors to return to the palace, saying that she would deal with the Barbarians alone, as she needed to vent her anger, tighten her bowstring, flex her forearm muscles, and stretch her leg nerves.

So she climbed the branches of that tree with her legs, standing on the edge of one branch and jumping to the edge of another, she continued climbing the branches until she disappeared among the leaves, then she released the arrow that pierced the man's chest. Although no one saw the arrow, she jumped to another tree and released another arrow. and so, within two seconds, arrows were falling from one tree after another in random order, causing confusion among the Berbers, as they could not deduce from which tree the next arrow would come. They thought they were being attacked by a fully equipped army of fierce soldiers, not by a single woman. Most of them took cover behind rocks and trees to protect themselves from the brutal attack, and it seemed that their plan had succeeded, as the attacks stopped for a moment. Then they saw that yellow meteor from the thunder strike a grassy spot and sink into it.

They did not understand the nature of that meteor, or that suicidal celestial body that fell near them, and they were afraid to approach it because of how many men they had lost. They looked around them cautiously, drawing closer to each other in panic and fear. Suddenly, that golden entity emerged from the ground and extended its left hand with a fiery spear that pierced a man's chest, then disappeared from whence it came. Two men rushed to where their colleague had fallen and bent down to examine the ground where the entity had disappeared. They found a hole leading to a narrow underground tunnel, barely big enough for a child, more like a snake's burrow than a tunnel. Before they could straighten their backs, the golden entity emerged from behind them and, with a sword in its right hand, severed their heads like apples. The men approached where their companions had fallen, and before they realised what was happening, they all fell, as arrows rained down from a nearby tree, striking them in the middle of their foreheads. The arrows hit those who were about to fight and spared those whose reactions were slowed by surprise. However, some of them managed to direct some of the arrows at the tree, but their arrows rebounded violently, falling close to them.

The men realised that they were being exterminated.

When only five of the fifty men remained, the golden projectile flew from the tree towards them. and she grasped her bloody spear with her left hand. For the first time, they heard her voice as she let out a battle cry that instilled in their hearts a fear they had never felt before. That cry bore fruit, for if any of them had intended to fight her before, they turned away from the fight after hearing that cry. However, one of them dared to raise his bow and aim his arrow at the head of that golden missile. She raised her sword with her right hand

and deflected the arrow in the air before she reached the ground. Then she turned her hand in a complex movement with infinite violence, precision and speed, the time interval between deflecting the arrow and changing its course was close to zero, and the arrow flew into the head of its owner, whose eyes widened in disbelief, and his death froze in that state of astonishment.

Before she reached the ground, her spear had lodged itself in the man's neck, protruding from the other side, and finally came to rest on the ground, not to catch her breath, but to stand still like a snow statue, for the three men to see her for the first time.

A vision of beauty, a masterpiece embodying splendour, her beauty paralysed them, she killed them with her eyelashes in this battle, and they were about to fall at her feet, but then they saw what she had done to their companions, and their animal instincts returned, along with their desire to survive. They raised their swords in her face. Their faces contorted with anger and contempt instead of admiration and awe.

They panted like wild dogs, and she stood silent as the grave. The three of them pounced on her at the same moment. She blocked the sword of the man who swung his sword at her head, then bent down, dove to the ground, and passed between his feet. She emerged from behind him as her sword spun around, the hilt in her hand and the blade pointing backwards. She plunged the sword into the man's back without seeing him and spun the sword violently horizontally to cut the man in two from the middle, his entrails falling onto the grassy ground.

The sword completed another horizontal rotation, severing the floating ribs of the second man, then another rotation, blowing away his rib cage, and a third rotation, blowing away his entrails. Then it rose at a frightening angle and fell on the sword of the last man, throwing him away. The unknown warrior looked at the man, whom the blood drained from his veins.

She approached him coldly and calmly, and he panicked and curled up into a ball.

8- THE SURVIVOR

She loved that effect. She may not have known she loved it, but she did. She could have killed him too with a wave of her blade, but she chose to keep him alive to gloat over him, to instil fear and terror in his heart, and to gain the great respect, fear and awe she deserved. She was the queen.

The queen who paved her way to the throne with blood, perseverance, strength and determination. And so she carefully wiped the blood that had drenched her sword from that man's jacket, carefully - on the sword - without caring about the man whose arm she had severed as she wiped the blood. Then she sheathed it in its place and went to where the spear was stuck in that fighter's neck and pulled it out in such a way that the fighter's head flew off and fell on the chest of the surviving man, who lost all his courage after the head of his comrade fell into his hands. She chose to instil all that fear in him.

"Who are you? What brought you to our province?"

"Will you-will you spare my life if I answer you?" he asked, stammered, between broken words.

"That depends on the answer," she replied coldly.

The man made up his mind and decided to tell her everything.

"We are the reconnaissance patrol exploring that beach, and we arrived yesterday from the area beyond the seas," he said.

"And which army do you belong to?" she continued her interrogation with the same coldness.

"To the army of the giant Berbers," he replied, as if ashamed of his answer.

"And what brought you here?" she repeated her question threateningly.

"We didn't mean to come here," he replied, waving his arms in terror, his voice trembling.

"We could not find this island on any map, even though we have every possible map. However, a fierce storm struck the ocean with such ferocity that we would have perished if we had not spotted this island from afar. We came here and camped in the northern village."

"How many of you are there?" she asked in a terrorising tone.

"I don't know exactly, hundreds, maybe a thousand or more. We are a large fleet. Even our commander may not know our exact number, with people joining us every day and leaving us every second," he replied honestly.

"When do you intend to leave?" she asked harshly.

The man remained silent, unable to answer.

"Answer me," she shouted in a rage that froze the blood in his veins and prevented it from reaching his heart, causing his pulse to quicken to compensate for the lack of blood

"We do not intend to leave before we have plundered the riches of this island. We are barbarians, we are thieves, murderers, looters, highwaymen," he replied fearfully.

"You are now in my province, and in my province things are different from anywhere else in the world. In my province, the only goal of men in life is food and procreation," she said calmly.

"Are we not all like that?" the man said in a natural tone, without humour.

"I mean that they are our food, and we exploit them sexually to procreate before we prey on them. On rare occasions, we keep them in pens like animals to do the menial tasks that we despise, such as cleaning up after the horses, planting, harvesting, and collecting waste," she said as if stating a fact, also without humour.

He opened his mouth in disbelief and said through his drooling saliva:

"What do you mean by exploiting them?" he asked.

"In your language, I mean we rape them," she explained harshly.

The astonished man's mouth opened wider as she continued:

"Don't worry, I'm not in the mood for meat right now, and you don't excite me in any way with your excessive weakness and flabbiness," she said.

"So I will relieve you of your misery immediately," she said, pointing the spear at his face.

"Wait! I answered all your questions very honestly," he said in panic and terror.

"But I didn't like your answers," she said coldly.

Before he had a chance to speak again, the spear plunged into his chest, bursting his troubled heart like a balloon.

She wiped the spear's blade on his jacket and walked coldly among the corpses of her victims without batting an eyelid. She appeared cold, harsh, brutal, violent, angry, tyrannical, powerful, self-confident, and formidable.

The sound of her metal boot heels rang out when they hit rocks, fell silent when they hit grass, and sank when they hit sand. She looked at the leather of her boots and the gold trim and shouted audibly:

"Damn it. The blood of these bastards has stained my clothes."

9- THE ENCOUNTER

After saying that, she ran on the tips of her shoes at breakneck speed, looking like a gazelle, then after hundreds of metres she climbed the branches of that tree and ran jumping between the branches like a monkey. After hundreds of metres, she pounced on that hole, whose location she knew well, and crawled between the cracks in the ground like a snake. Then she came out of that hole and continued running until she reached the island's shore. She stayed there, jumping headfirst and doing acrobatic moves on the sand until she flew like a small bird and landed in the water. For a whole minute, she remained motionless in the water, as if time had stopped for her.

Finally, she surfaced and began to swim, swim, swim, until the traces of blood disappeared, and she began to return from whence she came, intending to return to the palace when she glimpsed that corpse floating on the water. She swam to where the body was floating on its back, and with a touch of her finger on the neck of the body, she knew that its owner was alive and that it was no longer a corpse. He was an unconscious man, and without thinking, she grabbed his shirt collar like a criminal and dragged him like a feather to the shore.

When she reached the sand, she dragged him a little, then carried him like a child and took him to a hidden place among the trees, surrounded by branches and hidden by leaves. She laid him down roughly on the ground, felt his soft hair with her fingers, and ran them through his scalp as if searching for something. She placed her index fingers under his eyebrows on his eyelids and shook her head as if she were reading a hidden message that he would not tell her while awake. Then she placed her palms on his cheeks, surrounding his ears, then placed her left hand on his heart and her right hand on his jugular vein, and nodded her head in understanding.

Then she pressed something on his neck, and he gasped and jerked violently. He woke up in confusion. As soon as his vision cleared and his gaze fell on her, he said absently:

"Am I dead? Am I in heaven now?"

"No, you are in hell, you wretch. Hell is more merciful than what you will see here, you miserable creature," she said harshly.

He understood her language, as it was one of those he was fluent in. He gazed at her with admiration he could not hide, his eyes filled with a hypothetical love he bestowed on all human beings without exception. He read in her eyes what she did not know about herself, and he knew about her personality what she herself would never discover.

For some reason, she seeks to break him, to feel powerful, and to impose her control over him, to feel dominant. She seeks this because of her deep inner feeling of weakness and oppression and her need for appreciation, validation, encouragement, acceptance and support. She thinks she is strong when in fact she is weak.

He is strong because he loves her. He does not love her with the emotional love that is commonly known, but with the human love that allows him to sacrifice himself for her. It is the love of a human being for another human being, not the love of a lover for his beloved. For some reason, he felt pity for her because her heart was too narrow to love, and it had turned dark black with vengeance, evil, anger, hatred, and resentment. His feelings and pity turned into tenderness in his gaze and words, and he said:

"I don't think so, for I am already in bliss, even if you think otherwise," he said.

"We will eat you alive, you wretch," she shouted angrily.

His smile did not waver, so she continued to terrify him:

"Of course, we will not eat you right away. First, we will gouge out your eyes, then we will cut off your limbs, so you can hear us eating them raw, while we roast the rest of your body over a low fire," she said.

"You speak of nothing more than death. It is merely a gateway to another, truer life. A gateway to eternity, where there is great comfort," he said calmly, without knowing where the peace came from.

She was about to slap him, but something she did not understand prevented her, so she contented herself with shouting:

"Fine, you bastard. I won't kill you now because I want to keep you strong for the next time I see you."

She turned him onto his stomach and took metal chains from her belt, tying him to the trunk of a giant tree, saying mockingly, "Wait for me until you see me next time."

"I'll look forward to that," he said, unable to explain the longing in his voice.

She looked at him with a gaze that tried to convey as much contempt, disgust and loathing as possible, but something prevented her from doing so.

She turned away like a ray of light, leaping onto a slippery rock and jumping from it as if it were a springboard to the tip of a nearby tree branch. She leaned on a distant tree branch and began running along the branches until she disappeared from his sight.

WHEN REALITY MEETS FANTASY
NARRATED BY THE WOMAN

10- A Girl Is Born

I looked at the grassy ground and remembered. I was born here, in this place.

Ah, ah, ah, ah, ah.

Mmmmmmmm.

What is this?! What has happened?!

I feel something new that I have never felt before.

Ah, I have come into existence.

My soul has entered that little foetus in that galaxy, in that planet, on that continent, in that country, in that neighbourhood, in that woman, whom I mean is my mother.

But what is this, Mother?! What is all this hostility?! What are all these painful, bloody memories laden with your blood?!

What is all this tension and anxiety that you are passing on to me in your blood?! I understood then. If I had been a boy, my fate would have been death. Burial alive in a grave. That was the fate of newborn boys in our female society.

There are three types of women in our society: the ugly, the warriors, and the old. When a girl is born ugly or weak, she joins the ranks of the ugly. When a girl is born beautiful and grows up, she undergoes several tests that determine whether she will join the ranks of the warriors if she passes, or the ranks of the ugly if she fails. Thus, the category of ugly women includes those who are physically unattractive and those who fail the warrior tests. In the end, when both the warriors and the ugly women grow old, they join the ranks of the elderly women. The three types are headed by the queen, who is the most distinguished among the warriors.

The core of our female society is based on the warriors; they are the ones who preserve our tribe and our existence. They are the strong, attractive ones who possess the talent for fighting, endurance, and patience. Their philosophy embodies the essence of the Amazons as united warriors who worked to isolate men from them in order to enjoy endless cruelty and unlimited tyranny.

The ugly ones take care of childbirth and child-rearing; they are our mothers, while we, the warriors, will never be mothers. They work in traditional professions necessary for life; they are the nurturers of young girls and the carers of the elderly; among them are bridesmaids and maids.

The elderly are divided into types according to their talents. Some practise wisdom, some record our history, some participate in manual professions, and some raise the younger generations, educating them, instilling in them a contempt for men, and planting cruelty in their stony hearts. The elderly women do not adorn themselves, but let their white hair hang loose, and we feel comforted when we touch the sweat on the palms of the workers' hands. We feel mentally refreshed when we sit at the feet of the wise women, seeking knowledge and insight, and we feel reassured when we melt into the arms of the nannies who are affectionate towards us. There is no longer any need for them to adorn themselves.

Only the warriors adorn themselves, but they do not do so to feel feminine.

There is no room for women to adorn themselves in a society of women who have refused to feel femininity within themselves. Rather, we adorn ourselves only to complete the required physical perfection, to feel absolute control, explosive power, visible perfection, and infinite self-confidence.

There is no place for men among us, nor is there room for them in our hearts. For us, men are a means of providing us with more girls to extend our lineage, as well as a means of entertainment or fresh human food for our stomachs.

My mother feared for my fate if I had been a boy, or if I had been ugly, but I was nothing but a charming child from an early age. They loved me from the moment I was born. I was everything an Amazon should be: flawless beauty, a strong body, flexible nerves, and solid muscles. I was skilled, strong, flexible, and muscular. I won everyone's admiration, and when the time came for me to take the warrior tests, I excelled in every test in a remarkable way.

11- The Warrior

The first test I underwent was to be thrown unarmed among four fierce armed men, and the task was simple.

"To prove your worth, bring me the corpses of four men in just four minutes. You are required to bring me the heart of the first, the lungs of the second, the liver of the third, and the jaw of the fourth."

I broke branches and stabbed them into the eye sockets, hearts, and throats, and removed the organs they wanted with my sharp nails. I threw what they wanted at their feet with my right hand while biting the arm of one of them which I was holding with my left hand, all within a minute.

The warrior who tested me was very impressed. She was the most experienced woman in the tribe in the art of combat, brutal in combat, and skilled in survival. I felt my uniqueness from the very first moment. When self-confidence reaches its peak, the impossible becomes simple, and when there is no difference between life and death, you no longer cling to life, and you become a thousand times stronger in any battle of any kind. When you devote your entire life to studying the moments that determine your existence between life and death, between defeat and victory, and when your focus reaches the point where you break free from the constraints of place and time and fall into another realm of purity and serenity, so that you rise above any obstacle, then you will realise how I dazzled everyone around me and how I fought like an Amazon.

We love each other deeply and despise the world to the utmost. The first part relieved us of the idea that we are evil, because we have the capacity to love, we are good, and the second part gave us justification for anger, hatred, eating the flesh of our enemies, and drinking their blood. The Amazon warrior loves her comrade and gives her loyalty, attention, and tenderness, while treating others with cruelty, brutality, and contempt. We have satisfied good in some way and satisfied evil in some way, so we waver between the two sides without belonging to either.

I glimpsed that lion sneaking between the trees, and I remembered the test of savagery. At that moment, the warrior said brutally, "Those who refuse to eat raw meat have no place among us."

And so they threw me into a dark pit and left me for days without food or drink. After I had been there for a long time, I don't know how long, they threw a hungry, predatory lion at me. We didn't wait long before it bared its claws, and I raised my spear. My long, swift spear was the first to pierce the lion's chest as it pounced on me. With the momentum of my hand and its pounce, the spear plunged into the lion's spine from below its neck to above its tail.

I stuck the spear into the ground, cut it into pieces with my sword, and ate its raw meat. Then they threw my female companions who had failed the savagery test at me, and I ate them all.

This was not the only test in which I encountered a lion. There was also the test of survival in the wild, where I had to overcome a huge lion and its lioness and fend off a swarm of all kinds of wild animals.

It started with the lion pouncing, so I threw myself to the ground to let it pass over me, then I stood up quickly to deliver a powerful kick before it could regain its composure to face me.

I spun around quickly, and when I was close enough to the lion, I raised my left elbow and jabbed it into the lion's stomach. I then completed my spin while pulling my sword from its sheath. When the turn was complete, my right hand plunged the sword into the lion's stomach, turning it a full turn to spill its entrails onto the grass and leave it dead.

I hid inside the dead lion's entrails and convinced its lioness that the bloating meant it was dead and rotting, as it was not breathing and was covered in blood. Even animals can be fooled by their instincts! I remained in this position for hours until the test was over. A thousand predators passed by me, but I did not know their number or their nature. I only heard howls, roars, meows, and noises of all kinds and shapes. I saved myself with that clever trick.

Every test has a purpose. The gut test ignites your savagery to deal with the human body in a bolder way, to break the barrier of fear of taking a life. The savagery test aims to increase the lust for fighting, the habit of bloodshed, eating raw meat, increasing your savagery, killing innocence, hardening your tender heart, and the survival test in the wild aims to enhance your ability to rely on yourself and survive in the wild without any outside help.

12- THE TESTS

There are surprise tests that you may not know how to pass, which are more like riddles that test your intelligence and wit. I remember one of them, the elevation test. I woke up to find myself on top of a mountain with a surface area of one square metre in the middle of the day when the sun was directly overhead. All I had with me was a quiver with a single arrow and a bow. I looked around and realised that I had to hit a thin rope 100 metres away, which would activate a pulley that would lower a wooden bridge, providing me with an escape route. This test undoubtedly highlights the importance of the arrow in Amazonian warfare.

And so I stood like a statue, drawing my bow, gauging the wind with my body, swaying with it, measuring the humidity with my skin, imagining its effect on the head and tail of the arrow, melting into the details of the arrowhead, becoming one with it physically and emotionally, so that I and it were the same thing, and I imagined the target two steps away from my eyes. At the right moment, when the wind calms down, my index finger and thumb release the arrow's tail, which flies off on its crooked path to hit the target. Finally, the rope is cut, the bridge falls, I began to cross the bridge, and when I reached the middle, the ropes connecting it to its two anchor points broke, and I found myself falling like a stone.

But I caught hold of a rope and took that circular path until I hit the side of another mountain. When I came to a complete stop, I began to climb the rope to the top of the mountain, and I saw that man cutting the rope with his sword. Before he could do so, I threw my sword at him, and it pierced his heart, and he fell from above. I continued my ascent, but before I could reach the top, I found myself falling... Someone had cut the rope after all.

I took out my small dagger and stuck it between the rocks of the mountain and began a difficult climb to find ten men at the top of the mountain.

I threw myself among them, kicking those I kicked, stabbing those I stabbed, punching those I punched, all in quick succession, which led me to end up standing among the corpses of the dead, eager for more, but then I heard the warrior congratulating me.

This was not the most difficult test. The most difficult test was getting rid of my closest friends. Such is the rule in this harsh society, where a girl naturally becomes close to another girl to be her confidant, companion, and solace in her loneliness, when the two girls finish their training journey, the testing phase begins, which will determine whether that girl will join the ranks of the warriors, the ugly ones, or the dead. The final test is to kill the creatures you love most, a test of killing emotion.

"Kill the woman next to you, your dearest friend. That girl must be eliminated so that the strongest girl remains in the end. In the end, only the strongest and fiercest survive," the warrior says coldly, addressing both of us.

I was standing next to her when she gave me that order. I was used to not thinking about life and death situations, so before the warrior could finish her sentence: only the strongest and fiercest survive, my sword had already cut my dearest friend's stomach in half!

It doesn't need much thought or hesitation. Hesitation causes death or wastes time of our lives, and the hesitant end up living a life of endless hesitation. If the opportunity arises, and you are able, and it is in your best interest, then why hesitate?

Hesitation cost my friend her life. Survival was for the least hesitant, the quickest of wit, the most focused on the warrior's words, on life in general, and the least ruled by emotion over reason.

Although this did not surprise me, it greatly astonished the warrior, as she did not imagine that I would carry out the task so quickly and so efficiently. She said, stunned:

"I hope you understand the purpose of that test. One does not need another to live, as you have all the strength, mind and feelings you need, so there is no need for someone to give you a sense of satisfaction, strength, attention or happiness. That person may make you happy at first, but they will easily hold the keys to your heart and may use their tongue to inflict the most psychological damage on you, or to expose your secrets and expose you to your enemies if they turn against you. Do not put yourself at the mercy of another person's feelings. Be strong. be independent, fear nothing, fear no one. You have everything you need, do not wait for another. Those innocent feelings of kindness and friendship, if they invade your heart, will weaken it and make it fragile, creating a terrible weakness in you that would remain incurable for the rest of your life if you do not end it with your own hand here and now."

She then looked at my friend with awe and respect, and she gave a signal, so two girls carried her body away to some place, and she said reverently:

"Your friend will have an Amazon warrior's funeral, as she passed all the tests except the last one. You must not be angry with yourself but know that your mission from now on is to protect our society of the Amazons. We value each other to the utmost and love each other greatly, but our fierce hearts must not be tainted by excessive love, for that would weaken us. So we love each other, but within limits, for deep down we do not mourn our dead, we only honour them as befits their honourable lives.

"Do you understand?" she asked.

"Yes," I replied solemnly.

"Good. I have recommended you to the leader. Your ceremony to join the ranks of the warriors will be in the evening," she said with satisfaction.

"So be it," I said firmly, but not without a hint of excitement.

I was crowned a warrior that same day in a grand ceremony filled with the drinking of enemy blood, the recitation of magic spells, and wild dances, gypsy dances that were a mixture of madness, cruelty, seduction, and brutality.

The old woman also removed my right breast to help me remember that I was no longer an ordinary woman, that I was more special than just a man, and to help me physically so that my arrows would hit their targets with great accuracy without any physical impediment.

13- THE OLD WOMAN'S INDOCTRINATION

I looked at the grass around me and remembered that this was where I had received my first practical teaching.

"My dear, listen to my words," she said.

I nodded to the old woman. She was the most experienced, knowledgeable, and perceptive of the elders, having lived through the era when our small community was first formed.

Now she was going to teach me the truths of life, so that they would pass from her lips to the mind of my heart and the heart of my mind without passing through my ears, where words are stopped by the wax of forgetfulness and confusion, or by the mind's scepticism, reflection, and scrutiny. Children believe everything, even if it is not true, and later find it difficult to believe the truth, even when they are certain of it. I grew up on that wisdom, and it became difficult for me to believe anything else, even in those moments when my mind wanders and I think about my life.

"My dear little one, we are not the only rational creatures in this life. There are other creatures, but they are inferior to us. They are called men. Men are exactly like us, but they differ from us in that they are less intelligent than we are," she said.

"Their desires control them, so they behave like animals and resort to violence as a solution to their problems or loneliness. They do not consider peaceful solutions or use dialogue. Men kill or become depressed; they do not reconcile or compromise," she continued calmly.

I felt the words rooting themselves inside me.

"Men are despicable creatures who walk the earth wreaking havoc, convinced that they are right in everything they do, and seeking in every way to control women, whether through violence, flawed logic, or hypocrisy. When they gain control, they do whatever they want," she said with apparent hatred.

"When we tried life without them, we rose above them and surpassed them in everything. We became incomparably better on every level. The only problem is that we need them to reproduce," she added in ecstasy.

"And so we keep some prisoners who have infiltrated our society, or we take some men from one of our conquests, to reproduce with them and extend our lineage. It is completely permissible to insult them, to humiliate them, to force them to work in shameful jobs, and to compel them to perform shameful acts," she said, gesturing with her hand.

"Everything is permissible when dealing with men, for as I have said, they are inferior creatures who have been given supreme authority by society. Only we have finally tipped the balance, and now we have the final say. Men here deserve nothing but contempt, humiliation, consumption, murder, or all of the above," she said.

I did not question her. Questioning felt like betrayal.

"Men do not deserve pity. Pity weakens the heart and corrupts the soul. There is no place for pity here. The world is a cruel place, and it is foolish to live kindly in an evil world. Enemies do not deserve pity," she continued, waving her hands to warn me.

"Strangers are enemies. Anyone who is not an Amazonian stranger, and anything that is not under your skin, does not deserve your trust. Everyone may be a liar. Everything may be a dream. The only thing that is certain is your existence, which you must preserve with all your strength," she said, continuing her wisdom.

"When did these brilliant ideas start? Were we isolated from men from the beginning?" I asked.

"No, my dear. We lived side by side with men, and the relationship between us was normal. Sometimes we quarrelled and sometimes we made up. We loved and hated each other. We lived life with its randomness and regularity, with its fate and our will," she said, recalling distant events.

"We were content with life at that time until a ship of wicked pirates came and landed on our island. A fierce war broke out between our men and them, which ended with the extermination of our men and the invasion of our homes," she continued.

I kept listening carefully. My only job at this stage is to absorb her knowledge fully.

"They taught us how to fight, how to suppress our good feelings, and how to unleash our bad feelings—anger, hatred, envy, and greed. Those murderous rapists are responsible for making us the strong people you see today," she said, swallowing her saliva.

"At first, we learned the art of seduction to trap and control them. Then we learned how to control them through their stomachs. We realised that control comes from instinct and emotion, so we isolated our own desires and feelings and controlled them using theirs, which they had not isolated," she said.

Her tone became more intense.

"We secretly learned to fight, studied magic, and drank blood so that our enemies would walk in our veins—to understand them better, to become more savage, to distance ourselves from human weakness, to increase our animalistic side, to lessen the feelings that weaken the heart, and to silence the philosophical thoughts that paralyse the mind. We ate brains to become wiser, hearts to become stronger, and eyes to become more perceptive. When the right day came, we destroyed some of them, ate some of them, and captured the rest to continue our magical experiments and our revenge. Whenever one of us thought of loving someone as she had loved her husband, she would go to the man she liked, beat him, insult him, restrain him, and ultimately treat him as an animal taken by force," she said.

She looked away. I kept my gaze at her face, swinging between her moving lips and wandering eyes.

"Men are a word that no longer means anything to us after they all died in that dark period. The result we cherish is that we became better, stronger, and more beautiful without them. The only problem was the survival of our unique society after we, too, would one day die. So every decade we brought in a new batch of men—to make them taste the same torment we tasted, to take offspring from them, to rape them by force, and finally to kill them and bury them in the men's cemetery, writing on each gravestone: 'Born here, loved here, died here,'" she said.

"Men are a means of entertainment. We look after them like sheep, feed them, enrich them, make them happy, and then eat them in the end," she said with relish.

The old woman continued her indoctrination, explaining the laws and traditions of the Amazons and imparting their ideas to the young minds of the new generation. When her words bore fruit, my training with the warrior began, and I showed unparalleled skill. This coincided with a meeting with the leader, who explained to us the methods of fighting, attack and defence tactics, and engagement techniques.

I glimpsed the western battlefield, where we learned the art of combat from the leader.

14- THE LEADER'S TRAINING

You see the leader and love her despite yourself, for her formidable self-confidence, for her deadly beauty, for the look in her eyes that pierces you and strips you bare as a newborn, for her excessive, superhuman strength.

You see her holding her horse's mane, her long black hair flying in all directions behind her head as she rides, and you shiver with ecstasy, wishing you could be like her, even if only in another life.

"Weapons are to Amazons what air is to living beings, and water is to fish, essential for life. And the first weapon of an Amazon," the leader said.

She waved her fist in the air.

"Her hand. Her hand can dive into stone, and her foot can crush rock. A weapon is not a weapon unless you know how to use it or when to use it. Use your bow and arrows for long distances, your sword and spear for short distances, and for very short distances, hand-to-hand combat. I mean, hands are for close range, hands are for what range?" she said.

"Hands for close range," we said emphatically.

"The surrounding environment is our playground. You must learn to move on branches as if they were smooth ground, dive into the earth as if it were water, and live underwater as if it were your own personal room," she continued, with all huge strength.

"There are traps set around our tribe to catch anyone who dares to approach, and the arrows of the sniper squad will kill any intruder before they take a single step inside our invisible boundaries. You are only safe because your comrades protect you against unknown dangers," she said.

Her tone turned to pride.

"The Amazonian pierces the water like a fish, rides a horse as if she and the horse were one creature, hides among the trees like a chameleon, burrows into the ground like a worm, runs through the air like a ray of sunlight, and leaps from branch to branch with the agility of a monkey, the lightness of a gazelle, and the jump of a frog," she continued.

Her enthusiasm reached its peak.

"Kill, slaughter. The moment you kill someone is the only real moment in the world of illusions we live in. Be angry. Let anger be what drives you in this life, for it will give you the strength you seek. It will drive you to achieve everything you desire. You will not rest, and you will work like a roaring engine until your time comes. Your life is the axis, and your path is your goal. Do not step aside, do not waver, and do not stray from it," she said.

The leader continued her words, and I passed my tests and became an Amazon warrior. It wasn't long before I met the old woman, the leader, and the warrior.

"She is more beautiful than she should be, so much so that even I was saddened by what my hands had done to taint her heart and cut off her breast," the old woman said.

"She is stronger than she should be. She fights with such natural instinct that she hardly needs a teacher," the warrior added.

"She is tougher than she should be. She was born to take charge and lead thousands with an iron fist," the leader continued.

I was unanimously elected by everyone to be the Amazon princess who would succeed the queen, and less than a year later, I assumed the position of Queen of the Amazons.

I saw the palace from afar, and I entered it, swallowing my memories, to seek to devour more memories that had not yet happened.

I found the leader on my way.

"Leader, go to tree 305, where you will find a man tied to its trunk. Bring him here, take passageway 942 through branches 999, and bring him back here using method number 6," I ordered the leader.

"Yes, Your Majesty," the leader muttered.

The leader wondered what that wretch had done to deserve the treatment our queen had ordered, method number 6.

"Bring the warrior here!" I called out to my first attendant.

"Yes, my Queen," she replied respectfully.

I saw the warrior, my subordinate now. She had been my teacher, and I held her in high esteem, but now she obeys me. Such is the law of life. I was more distinguished than her, despite the fact that she had come into this life before me.

"Go to location 550-30, where you will find a number of dead men. Dig up their bodies to get what you need from them, and take a platoon of Class C with you," I ordered the warrior.

"Understood," she shouted enthusiastically.

I continued on my way until I ascended the throne. I remember those glorious moments when I bathed my body in blood and then danced that frenzied dance, which is an essential part of the coronation ritual. Blood must be shed to crown a queen, and I try in vain to push that insolent man out of my mind. I will break him, I will humiliate him, I will insult him to the utmost. Let him wait for me and see what will become of me. Despite myself, my thoughts and my eighth sense, I found myself compelled to go to where I had bound him.

PRESENT MOMENT
NARRATED BY THE MAN, AGAIN

15- THE PRISON

I contemplated the beautiful nature around me. All beauty requires is an eye to notice it. I stayed among the crops, water and trees, uniting with the green leaves, blessed in their dew, and breathing in the fresh air. It is true that I am bound, but this does not prevent my skin from enjoying this wonderful atmosphere, nor does it prevent my nose from breathing in that fresh air, nor does it prevent my cheeks from smiling at that breathtaking nature.

Then I glimpsed that ship on the horizon.

Then I saw them coming from afar.

Bare shoulders, bare legs, a golden piece covering the chest, a golden piece covering the waist, small golden shoes covering the feet, golden bracelets covering the forearms and wrists, golden ribbons intertwined with golden yellow hair.

They are thirty women, seemingly charming in appearance, seemingly deadly in their equipment and weapons, and they are heading towards me as if they know my exact location.

They reached me, the first one slapped me, then the rest rained down slaps on me, and when they finished, I felt the heat wash over me from the speed, force and focus of the blows. I closed my eyes from the intense pain and refused to let my tears fall, struggling to do so.

My bonds were loosened, and I fell to the ground. One of them had untied me, and she placed her foot on my chest to stifle my breathing. It was as if that humiliating gesture gave the others permission to kick me. Then that warrior appeared, riding that horse, and threw the rope to another who tied my feet to the end of the rope. No sooner had she done so than the rider set off on the horse, dragging me across the sand, filling my mouth with sand as the horse trampled the desert sand. Then the thorns cut me as the horse devoured the forest grass.

My vision was clouded by the intense pain and the thorns, dust, sand and grass that had entered my eyes. The horse stopped, and then soft hands carried me with such force as if they were the hands of a giant and I was Thumbelina and moved me to some place. After a few moments, they threw me onto a cold, damp stone floor. I opened my eyes, but they did not function, or perhaps the pitch darkness they had thrown me into did not allow me to see even my own hands. Then I felt chains around my legs and heavy metal chains wrapped around my feet and hands, suffocating my breath.

I was bound in an internal, dark, windowless, doorless prison.

Of course, I did not know that the coast guard had informed the queen moments after spotting the ship heading for the island, and that a death sentence had been issued in absentia for the poor passengers of the ship, which was nothing more than an expeditionary vessel searching for life on that unknown island that did not appear on any map. After the ship docked, the scientists and trackers immediately set to work, and when they finished, a battalion of one hundred fighters decided to penetrate the forest in the hope that it would lead them to an inhabited village or an unknown tribe. And so the battalion entered the forest accompanied by the team of scientists and trackers.

The members of the exploration battalion walked slowly through the grass, and in an instant, dozens of arrows fell from among the leaves of the tree branches, each arrow hitting its target. The targets of the arrows were the men's chests, and at the same moment, the ground split open and spears pierced the men's stomachs. Those who remained faced the surprise of their lives in the next second.

Those who lived in the trees descended from the sky, and those who were buried in earthen pits emerged from the ground. They wielded their swords and daggers at the chests, throats, and legs of the men, few of whom defended themselves from those who overcame the shock of the surprise. The men's huge shields faced the women's sharp spears, and the shields collapsed under the weight of the spears, shattering into small pieces.

An Amazon throws a dagger at a tree, then quickly ascends to where she has stuck it, hugging the branch with her legs, while she takes out her bow and arrows and shoots her enemies. She descends from the tree headfirst and returns to it with ease. She does all this using a dagger tied to a thin, invisible rope. The long grasses hanging from the tall trees wrap around the waists and stomachs of her enemies, tightening around them and keeping them suspended between heaven and earth like animals awaiting slaughter.

A savage smile of joy, lowered upper eyelashes, arched eyebrows, pursed and stretched lips, wild hair, focused eyes—the Amazons are at war.

These Amazons are living a beautiful moment, defending their existence in that cruel world, defending their land, their femininity, and their very existence to the last breath. They have instilled fear and terror in the hearts of men and tipped the scales of life after changing the course of destiny. They live for each other, not for themselves, for an Amazon cannot betray her fellow Amazon. They satisfy their instinct for survival, their lust for battle, their desire for revenge, their feelings of hatred, and their wish for destruction. They eat the flesh of their enemies and do whatever they want in the name of preserving themselves and each other, in the name of a higher female cause, and in the name of laws made just for them.

In less than a minute, the expedition was completely wiped out. They will surely say that their ship was destroyed or swallowed by the ocean. Rumours will spread that they died in mysterious circumstances. Everything is over, the matter is settled, and my hope of rescue is lost before it even began.

I felt extremely exhausted and terribly tired, so I surrendered to sleep despite myself.

16- THE HUMILIATION

When I woke up, I did not know if the sun had risen or not, as the darkness that prevented me from seeing my hands had not yet lifted. However, despite everything, a smile of satisfaction spread across my face, for it was a new day, and a new day is a new opportunity for new hope and new happy events.

When the pages are filled with all those lines and letters, perhaps the only possible solution is to turn the page to a blank page, a new day.

My hands are bound, but my will is free. My eyesight is impaired and my eyes are veiled from the light, but my vision is still there. My body is confined to a specific place, but my imagination is set free. My head is fixed in place, but the thoughts that spring from my mind can move as they please in any direction.

They will not prevent my imagination from moving as it pleases in any direction and in any way. I closed my eyes tightly, left that place, boarded that ship, breathed in the fresh morning air, dipped my hands in the cold water, and felt its soft texture tickling my hands. When the ship docked, I went to our house and threw myself into my mother's arms.

An embrace is a means of containment, a way of expressing love, tenderness and care.

The embrace of a lover who gives you love, the embrace of a father who gives you security, the embrace of a mother who makes you feel tenderness, the embrace of a child who makes you feel care, the embrace of a friend who makes you feel accompanied, the embrace of creation that makes you feel alive, the embrace of God that makes you feel existence.

I experienced all those in silence, with people I used to know in my imagination. Then I went to my friends and talked to some of them. I told them what I wanted to say, and I imagined what they might say in response to those words. When you know someone well, you can always know what they might do in certain situations, what their thoughts are, and the nature of their feelings, so you feel them alive within you with all their words, reactions, and actions.

Then I walked along the bank of that river, stretching my legs, and I imagined the water, drawing it with my eyes closed. Then I moved the waves with my breath, turned on the radio, and listened to that song. I memorised it, repeating it in my imagination without it coming out of my mouth. It echoed in my ears with its singer's voice. Then I found that tape that I had never listened to before, and I listened to it, putting the words and melodies together randomly as I pleased.

I drank my favourite drink and ate my favourite meal, and finally, when I realised there was nothing new to do, I returned to reality, because despite everything, I preferred reality to illusions.

After a period of time, the length of which I do not know, I felt a hand pushing me to the ground, another hand slapping me, another tearing my clothes until I was completely naked, and two hands completely restraining my movements. Then I felt that woman forcibly having sex with me. I screamed, and then that powerful slap fell on me. I shouted in anger and rebellion:

'No...'

My scream was lost in the depths of silence, darkness and stillness. More than one woman took turns raping me with relish, lust and control on their part, and with anger, rage and agitation on my part. They broke me.

Yet again, there was something exciting about it, I wouldn't dare to face or acknowledge. It's wrapped deep in the human psyche with a thousand locks, behind a hundred masks, beneath ten veils, in complete darkness, at the bottom of the deepest ocean.

The devil trinity of lust, greed and ego is manifested in one act. The ego lusts in the form of bodily pleasure. The egoic nature to pleases itself, is self-worship through pleasure. The greed is manifested in desire to possess material things and human beings through imposing power, dominance and aggression. Where sex and violence collide, they produce power exchange through sex, though nonconsensual, involuntary and unintentional, yet it brought me to the same place.

There's an assorted lot of contradicting emotions there. There are love and attention, embracing abuse and contempt, acceptance meets rejection, pull synchronises with push, physical pleasure starts to associate with emotional humiliation, forming new neural pathways in the brain, which taint all the guilt of my sins and the shame of others abusing me with erotic pleasure, which makes humiliation a gateway to pleasure, which makes the sexual abuse passing from the physical realm to the psychological realm of thoughts and emotions.

I have only my spirit to seek healing and reverse the process; by healing the psyche and then the latter heals the body.

That woman came and blocked the air from my lungs. I was suffocating. I couldn't move, but I was aware of everything that was happening to me. They humiliated me, wounded me, drew my blood, and drank it with relish.

Finally, they left me. I trembled a thousand times and shook a thousand times. The darkness surrounding me frightened me in a mythical way. I imagined a snake attacking me, a crocodile tearing my head off my body, and a tiger devouring my chest. The darkness that engulfed me was like drowning your soul in the depths of endless, dark, eternal space, with no control on your part, or like drowning in the deepest ocean at the darkest hour of the night.

And so, without warning, without a fixed schedule, at random times, on any given day, the blows rain down on me, and then some women rape me. They deliberately leave me alive each time. They enjoy torturing and humiliating me, and they rejoice in my weakness and my oppression.

17- THE SECOND ENCOUNTER

That night, light shone in my eyes for the first time in days, or months, or that indefinite period of time, and I saw the queen, looking at me with sadistic pity.

She had succeeded in breaking me, that was certain.

The Amazons took turns raping me, and I looked at their queen, bleeding rivers of shame, my pride wounds swelled, my heart bleeding, crushed by the feet of the Amazons, bare and dry as the edge of a sword. I cry without tears, not because my dignity has imprisoned my tears, but only because my tears are too many to come out into existence. I suffer from those moments when one is on the verge of a nervous breakdown.

It is that bitterness that fills your mouth, preventing you from opening it at all, and pushing the blood in your arteries so fast that it burns your veins, and you feel the heat overwhelming you, your pulse quickening, and a violent emotion sweeping you away, leaving you with nothing but killing and destruction to vent that intense emotion.

But no, their evil will not succeed in overcoming my goodness, and negative feelings will not succeed in overcoming positive feelings. They are just respectable human women who behave like animals, not because they are animals, but only because they know no other way of life. Despite myself, I found myself looking at their queen, and I smiled with pity for her. It is true that she appears to be in a position of strength, and I appear to be in a position of weakness, but I felt her helplessness, which drove her to behave in this terrible way. I pitied her and her situation, which keeps her heart torn, her spirit scattered, and her mind polluted.

She raised her hand in a certain gesture, and one of them extinguished the torches that lit up the place. Then those who were sitting on my chest left me and walked away. Then I felt hot breath on my bare chest, and I heard her say in a deep voice:

"Why are you looking at me like that? Don't you fear me, man?!" she said.

It was the queen speaking to me in the heart of darkness, so I replied, "Should I?!"

Her tone became sharp as she said, "Of course. Don't you know what I can do to you?!"

"More than you've already done?!" I asked in surprise.

"Yes, more than I've already done. I only asked them to do the light stuff, and I never told them to eat you like an evening dessert, piece by piece, every day, saving your head as the last piece," she said simply.

"Why didn't you do it?!" I asked without fear.

My question was normal, and I expected a violent response from her, but her reply came in a tone dripping with confusion:

"I don't know. I didn't even care to be the first to kill you, as tradition dictates. I couldn't, for reasons unknown to me. I don't know why I'm talking to you now either. My hesitation before coming to you is also unknown. My hesitation in ordering your death is completely unknown."

She was surprised by her human feelings and her innate kindness. It was the right time to explain the truths of the universe to her, and so I stayed and talked to her, and she talked to me. That meeting ended, and we had many more meetings after that, during which I learned everything about her, and she learned everything about me. During these meetings, I noticed my intense admiration for her, and she felt something attracting her to me, but she resisted it fiercely.

I set about demolishing the fortresses of evil entrenched in her heart, to free her heart from the bondage of hatred, by all means, all the time. Then, during one meeting, one day, I said to her:

"This is why we were created, my dear, to care for each other, to love each other, and to be kind to each other. If a single drop of hatred enters our loving hearts, it is enough to corrupt the whiteness of our entire hearts and stain them black. In other words, if you hate one person, it is enough to corrupt your entire heart," I said.

"Ha! No way! Anger is the answer, hatred is the solution, revenge is the way. Are you crazy? Don't you know the strong when you see them? We are strong with these principles and this way of life," she shouted sarcastically.

"Strength lies in forgiveness, in giving without expecting to receive, and in loving others when they hate you. Weakness lies in returning hatred for hatred, in giving in to feelings of revenge, and in succumbing to your animalistic desires for killing, eating, and sex. It is easy to get angry, to kill. It is difficult to forgive, to heal the broken, and to treat the sick," I explained.

"That's backwards logic, only you see it that way. People don't fear those who think that way, they fear people like me," she said confidently.

"Why do you make people fear you?!" I asked defiantly.

"In pursuit of respect," she replied immediately.

"But they respect you out of fear, not love, and their fear itself will drive them to trample you when they have the weapon, the opportunity, and the time. Who wants respect that comes from fear, not awe and love?!" I said, contradicting her idea.

"You speak of love in a place that does not recognise it. We do not follow your school of thought, O man. Our school is one of revenge and hatred, not forgiveness and love. Do you want us to preserve our identity with love? Who will defend our society?" she said in retreat.

"Love will preserve your happiness and your good reputation, while revenge will dig a grave for each of you before it digs graves for your enemies," I persisted.

"It is your grave, you fool, that will soon cover you. Don't you know how to hold your tongue among your enemies? Isn't it foolish to say such things to me when you are my prisoner? You are nothing but a rejected odd slave in my kingdom," she said angrily.

"Love gives me needed confidence and courage to express what I feel and believe without fearing anything. Fear is the result of hatred, war and revenge, and security is the result of a life of love, peace and forgiveness," I smiled peacefully and calmly.

"Let love give you the courage to face death. We will celebrate your death in the middle of the night tomorrow," she shouted in anger.

She left angrily after setting the date of my death in that friendly meeting.

I will have to wait for my death. I still believe that there is wisdom behind all this. Until now, I have not acted wrongly in any of the situations I have faced, and as long as I have not acted wrongly, what is happening to me is good. I just have to wait, even if my death is the right thing.

How cruel that queen is! No, no, I will not condemn her. I will not take on the responsibility of God, who has not condemned her now. He sees her and is patient with her until she dies. I will not do so now, and I will not condemn her, lest she repent and I remain a sinner who dares to sit in the seat of God the Judge. If I begin to condemn her, I will find no excuse to help her, no strength to comfort her, and no time to love her.

Despite everything, I am still grateful for what has befallen me, and I am amazed at my gratitude in such circumstances!

18- THE EXECUTION

Tomorrow will come, inevitably. It is a great blessing that we do not know the time of our death. It is truly better to suffer misfortune than to wait for it. Those were feverish moments I spent knowing that I would die tomorrow. How many situations I left behind! How many words I should have said but did not utter! How many deeds I should have done but did not even come close to doing! Suddenly and without warning, the curtain will fall on the play of my life, and the world will not stand helpless after me, but will continue as it was before me.

One thinks that, one is the centre of the universe and that all people and things are there to serve and comfort one, but one is shocked when one dies and finds that nothing has been affected. Some will shed a few tears for a while, that's all, and even if some shed tears all the time until they die, it will end with the end of their lives and the end of that dear one they mourn inside them with their death.

I will die tomorrow, and despite everything, that strange body demands that I sleep today, and I fell asleep. I slept.

Tomorrow came, it was coming whether I liked it or not, I cannot stop time just because I do not like tomorrow, but how can I be sure that the sun rose in this complete darkness, it is just a hunch, and how will I know when midnight is in this way, I will surely go mad before they take me out to execute me.

So be it, let it be.

What would I do if time turned back?

I kept thinking, and before the answer came to me, time stole me away.

Soft hands grabbed my collar roughly, and violent hands broke the chains that bound my movements. Strong hands stood me up harshly and dragged me through corridors, roads, staircases and gates. Finally, they stopped me in front of a seat encrusted with gold and diamonds in a spacious hall and left me free to move, naked, cold, frozen, bleeding, bruised and broken, and then they left.

Then I saw her, and my heart fluttered despite everything.

Standing like the moon, on a pitch-black night, bathed in light.

Something in her eyes and eyelashes calls out to you and challenges you, provoking the man in your veins, saying, 'You will not have me, you will not break me. you are too weak to do so, and I am too strong to let you.' Something in her confidence, her pride, and her self-esteem stirs you, rushes you, overwhelms you, and delays you. She is no ordinary woman; she is a queen.

And she was indeed a queen.

And I was an ordinary man, even more ordinary than I should have been. I was nothing to her, a nobody, an indefinable quantity.

She is a queen, and I am a wounded man lying on the ground.

She is the hunter, and I am the prey.

I must accept the verdict of death with resignation, for we will all die one day, and if death is inevitable, let us die with a smile on our faces, for there is nothing worth frowning about.

She made a gesture with her hand that must have meant something, but nothing happened. I saw an angry, repulsive, astonished, and disapproving look on her face, and she repeated the gesture, but nothing happened. Suddenly, twenty Berbers stormed in, their chief laughing.

"They are not here to hear you, Queen. They are in another world," the chief said.

In the blink of an eye, she drew her bow and killed five of them. Her spear flew like a nail, striking two of them at once into the stone wall, then the dagger settled in the forehead of one of them, just as four of them restrained her from behind, one on each limb.

Her nerves tightened, then suddenly relaxed, then tightened again, and she broke free from them, breaking the bones of the neck of the one holding her with her right hand and the bones of the arm of the one holding her with her left hand. She fell to the ground on her hands,

kicking those who were holding her legs, but others crouched on top of her, bound her with chains, and another planted a thin needle in her arm, and her movements subsided despite herself.

"How?!" she screamed with what remained of her consciousness in a daze.

"We lost ten men for every one of your warriors, but we have no regrets. We studied your hiding places underground among the cracks, on the ground among the grass, and above ground on the branches of trees, and we concluded that the most appropriate way to penetrate your impenetrable defences was with a brutal attack. And so I entered with all my forces, knowing that I would lose most of my men, and that only a few would remain with me, enough to destroy you and continue on my way," the Berber chief replied proudly.

He looked at me with a scrutinising gaze tinged with contempt.

"Fighters have no value to us; they are mercenaries after all. We are barbarians who owe allegiance only to ourselves and our stomachs. Let those who are lost be lost. What value does a single person have in this crowded life teeming with so many people? A primitive fighter can be tricked and persuaded that he will survive as he goes to his death, and for that reason, I do not consider your beautiful head a loss, even if it means losing a thousand fighters. Your captivating head is worth it," he continued with a sneer.

"When I saw you fighting like that, I knew that you were worth a thousand fighters, and that if I struck the shepherd, the sheep would scatter, and everyone would be lost with the loss of the symbol, the symbol of your tribe, the symbol of your ideas, the essence of your society, and this symbol is concentrated in that head," he continued with malice.

He took an axe from behind his back and raised it high in the sky.

"Wait! Wait, my friend!" I shouted

He looked at me suspiciously and stopped.

"You must not kill her, or you will be cursed by the Amazons. Haven't you read the book The Magic of the Amazons?" I continued

"No, I haven't," he said, doubt creeping into his voice.

"You should have, my friend, before you commit this foolish and reckless act," I said quickly.

He looked at me with angry questioning eyes.

"Neither you nor any of your warriors or clan members should kill her, because if you do, you and the rest of the clan will die, as whoever kills the Amazon queen will be exterminated along with his clan before the sun rises the next day," I said indignantly.

"Are you serious?!" he asked harshly.

"Do I look like I'm joking?" I asked.

"Why are you telling me these facts now? Why are you helping me?" he asked harshly, tinged with suspicion.

"Maybe I'm that woman's friend! No, my dear, I don't have any feelings for that woman that would allow me to say what I'm saying," I said sarcastically.

Then I quickly continued in a sincere tone:

"Because we have a common enemy. Look at my situation, man, look at what she did to me and see for yourself. I am saying what I am saying for my own benefit, as I want her to die irrevocably, with no loss to her killers," I said sincerely.

He thought for a moment, then made up his mind.

"So be it. I cannot think of a solution to this dilemma now. I will take her prisoner for now and think about it later," he said.

And so he left me and walked away.

19- THE NOBODY AND THE QUEEN

"Wait for me. I am a stranger here. I am not one of your clan, nor one of your men, nor of your blood, but if you leave me here, they will kill me. Take me with you. I just saved your life," I said.

"No, I will not. Die, or live. It is enough that I did not kill you," he said harshly.

Then a man leaned over and whispered something in the ear of the chief, who seemed to be his deputy. The chief straightened up.

"Very well, you will come with us, but in your poor condition, you may die quickly. If you die, we will not help you, nor will we do anything to prolong your life. Let fate decide your destiny," the chief said.

"" the deputy said.

The deputy leaned over to whisper in the chief's ear again. I couldn't heat the deputy, but I think he is on my side for some reason.

"We do not help our wounded. Let those who are too weak to live die and let those who are unable to exist perish," the chief shouted at the deputy.

He addressed one of his fighters, pointing at me

"Take him!" he commanded the fighter.

The man carried me and placed me under his horse's legs. He waited until everyone had gathered, then sat me on the horse's back, mounted his saddle, and set off with the procession carrying the Berber chief, the Amazon queen, and dozens of Berber fighters.

On the saddle of that horse, I noticed an axe placed in a sheath on the saddle, as well as a jar containing some grain, probably used to feed the horse. A giant sword and an imposing shield were also hanging on the saddle.

The procession moved with awe, majesty, speed, and violence befitting the abduction of the queen. The speed at which the procession moved caused a violent vibration on the horse that my bruised bones could not withstand, and I found myself falling from the horse's saddle and hitting the ground with force. I heard someone shouting at the man:

"Leave him, let's go."

It was all over. I would die here, and I would lose the queen.

No, I won't lose her. I will save her. I opened the jar of grain before I fell, when I felt my balance falter and my body sway. I will save her even if I die. I will save her, and then I will die. And so I looked at the grain that formed a line on the grassy ground, and I contemplated it with my eyes, concentrating to distinguish it.

And I followed it.

Crawling, moving with my hands, leaving pieces of my flesh torn by thorns on the ground, watering the grass with my warm blood, transferring the heat of my bones to the soil like an exploding volcano meeting an icy pond.

I continued to crawl slowly, and it seemed as if my crawl would go on forever.

My mind stopped working, and I became a machine, so much so that I did not feel the passage of time. I may have crawled for an hour, two, three, or more. The end result was that I finally reached the place where they had tied the queen to a tree in the centre of a space where they had cut down all the trees around it. The tree to which the queen was tied looked like a dot in the centre of a vast empty circular space, which ended where the trees began again. I caught sight of a number of Berber fighters circling that empty space, glaring at the queen in steady patrols.

If I wanted to save her, I had to resort to trickery. I looked around me, searching for something that could help me, but found nothing but trees. There were empty containers of the fossil fuel that had once carried. I spotted a number of horses tied to a nearby tree.

An idea came to me, the only reasonable one in my circumstances. I crawled to the horses and gathered all the swords, axes and daggers, then moved from tree to tree, gently cutting the bark and extracting the liquid that came out of it. I put it in the containers after adding some of the herbs. When I was done, I placed the four containers at four equal points around the perimeter of the circle surrounding the queen. Then I took up the largest sword and stood watching the guard patrols, observing them to see when they disappeared, why, and how long they remained away from their posts.

I poured the first container and moved it in a quarter circle, filling the entire arc with liquid, until I found the second container and poured its contents into a new quarter circle.

No sooner had I finished than I poured the third container to fill the third quarter circle. When I finished, I poured the last container, filling the last quarter circle, but I left myself enough space to cross over to the queen. When the right moment came to move, I moved towards the queen, and when I reached her, I struck her shackles once with my sword. No one noticed. The second time, the sound caught someone's attention. The third time, it caught the attention of another. They were heading towards us. The fifth time, however, the glue I had extracted from the trees and poured around the circle surrounding us kept them in place, helpless like fierce dogs tied with chains. Sixth, seventh, eighth, and ninth strike I stroke with the sword, she regained her consciousness, and on the twentieth strike, the ring I was striking, the weakest link of the chains she was hanging on, broke, and my strength gave out.

I was surprised to see her carry me like a child in her arms and fly me over a nearby tree branch. Then she jumped off it violently to mount that horse, taking the sword from me with ease and cutting the rope that tied the horse to the tree. She set off with me on the horse, racing against time and the wind, with angry shouts echoing behind us, warnings and threats, the clang of swords and the dust of anger reaching our ears.

My mind cleared, and I came to my senses, amazed at the strength that had come over me to save her. The strength that left me after I had saved her, only for her to flee and help me escape, and save us both from the clutches of the Berbers. I gazed at her closely, at her white skin and golden hair, and I was lost.

I did not lose consciousness at that moment, but I lost my unconsciousness.

20- The Escape

I loved her. I only realised this when I was in danger. It was then and only then that feelings of longing and tenderness awakened in me, ignited in my heart, and prompted me to act and save her in that way.

Why did I love her? I don't know. One loves without thinking about why one loves one's beloved. It is true that one sets criteria for the girl of one's dreams, but many girls possess the same characteristics that one desires. So what drives one to choose that girl over others? The strangest thing is that he may love a girl who is far from the specifications he has set. Why her? She is the opposite of him and the opposite of the image he has painted in his imagination of his girl!

If you ask someone: What do you love about your beloved? they would often be unable to answer, or they might give you an answer that is missing something that they themselves do not realise. A person may love someone who sympathises with them, encourages them or showers them with attention, or, on the contrary, they may love someone who mistreats them, despises them and does not care about them, or they may love a beautiful, elegant woman, or they may love when the pain of loneliness cries out and pushes them to love another, or they may love when the time is right, or when their beloved is the only one available among the rest of the girls. Any circumstances and events can create a love story between two lovers on the stage of life.

I do not know why I loved her, whether for her beauty, her self-confidence, her outlook on life, her strength, or because she had never loved before. Or did I love her because I knew her depths and saw inside her, certain that despite all her outward appearances, she was a beautiful, gentle, and compassionate person?

Did I love her like a doctor loves a patient, or a teacher loves a student, because I took it upon myself to teach her the proper principles of life? Or did I love her like a slave loves his mistress, or a servant loves his owner, after she broke me so badly? Did I love her because I talked to her a lot, or because I was around her a lot, or perhaps because I had never loved anyone else before her, or because she was different from everyone I had ever known? I do not know why or how I came to love her! All I know is that I love her with a love that words cannot describe and meanings cannot express.

I looked at her to find that, for the first time she looked at me with that tender gaze.

"Why did you save me, you wretch?! I was about to kill you when the Berbers stormed the place?! Why did you do what you did?!" she said harshly.

"Don't you really know?" I said weakly, as that short battle had drained me of all my strength.

"Do you think I would know the answer and ask at the same time?" she said with a mocking cry of surprise.

"And you don't feel the answer?" I said, looking into her eyes.

She turned her face away.

"That's what amazes me the most. I grew up believing that men are insects, stupid animals, lustful dogs, sticky parasites, creatures inferior and uglier than our gender, who intrude on us. We surpass them in everything: intelligence, beauty, agility, and strength," she said in confusion

I was amazed at how men dominated women outside of that island where we had changed the status quo! But now, for the first time, I feel strange new emotions overwhelming me, sweeping me away, emotions I cannot understand. I see you differently from how I described men," she continued.

She smiled and looked me in my eyes then. I didn't deviate my gaze at her eyes. She kept explaining her situation:

"I didn't know these strange feelings existed before, and the wise old woman who taught me the wisdom of life and the laws of existence never told me about them."

She then looked away as if she was recalling a distant memory as her smile slowly disappeared, as she continued:

"All she told me about was the physical relationship that leads to procreation. She only talked about instincts. Those feelings prevented me from hitting you or insulting you or being the first to humiliate you according to our customs. Those feelings prompted me to treat you in the worst possible way, as I felt that you had some kind of effect on me that weakened me in some way and threatened my peace of mind in a way I did not understand. It prompted me to distance you from me as much as possible, so I moved you to the furthest cell in the depths of our prisons, to spare my eyes from seeing you. "

"I was confident that your intelligence would lead you to the conclusion on your own without anyone else telling you. It is our human instinct that gives rise to that selfless, sacrificial, and generous love. I never doubted your intelligence," I said brightly.

"Love is not a term that is used here," she said, shaking her head forcefully.

"Why?" I asked.

"Some men are not worthy of love," she said.

"Not all men are the same," I said.

"We were created this way to punish men," she said, clenching her fist.

"Women are not complete without men," I said calmly, pointing my index finger.

"We are not complete with these animal-like creatures," she said with disgust.

"Not all men are animalistic, lustful creatures. There are compassionate and loving men, there are rational men, and there are spiritual men," I said simply.

"The world is a harsh place, and there is no room for the tenderness you speak of," she said fiercely.

"Love is not a matter of choice, nor is it a luxury enjoyed by some; it is a necessity of life and a fundamental commandment," I said with a smile.

"Those feelings have made me weak and filled my heart with fear for the first time! For the first time in my life, I feel vulnerable!" she continued in the same fierce tone.

"Love, my dear, is not weakness, but strength," I said, pleased with her admission.

"Tell that to the weakness that overwhelms me and engulfs me whenever you look at me," she said stubbornly.

"Love is a brute force, and when guided by the mind, it is a rational force, and when led by the spirit, it is a powerful, boundless rational force. Don't you see what I have been able to do just because I love you?" I said emphatically.

When you love, you do not care whether you live or die for the sake of the one you love, not out of anger and hatred for life, for the love of life reaches the highest possible degree but does not precede the love of the beloved and the love of people. Both ways will give you the strength you need for war and for life, but love brings with it comfort, peace and stability, while anger brings with it fear, turmoil and boredom," I continued.

"And fear?!" she asked sceptically.

"It is not fear, but rather a feverish concern for another person, you feel affection for them and wish for them to be happy, content, free from harm and in excellent condition. You love someone so much that you fear for them from the air around them. You may fear your actions might hurt them, and you strive to be the image they desire. This is the most wonderful thing about that emotion, as you unknowingly transform yourself into a better person than you are now."

She seemed convinced.

"Why do you live? What is your purpose in staying alive?" I asked with genuine interest to know the answer and to confirm the point we were discussing.

"I live for problems and difficulties," she replied quickly, "not for luxury and comfort. Difficulties are what give life the meaning and challenge necessary for survival. I live to keep our society clean and unpolluted. I break others so I can feel my strength. I devour others so I can feel their blood in my veins and double my humanity. I oppress others so I can feel my power and authority."

" If others who are wrong always think they are right, and if you think you are right, isn't it possible that you are wrong in what you think?" I asked

"Wait! What did you say?!" she asked in surprise.

"I simply mean, isn't it possible that you are wrong in what you think?!" I explained.

"About what?!" she asked.

"About your laws. Strength is not in breaking, but in mending; greatness is not in domination, but in submission; wisdom is not in war, but in peace; difficulty is not in revenge, but in forgiveness. How do you know that the laws you have committed yourselves to are correct?!" I replied.

"Practical experience has proven their validity," she replied simply.

"But you have never seen a way of life other than the one you live by," I said.

"Life is not easy, as you say," she said with a hint of weariness.

"Life is easy for those who see it as easy and complicated for those who see it as complicated. Life is a joyful journey for those who see it as joyful, a dangerous adventure for those who see it as dangerous, harsh for those who see it as harsh, and tender for those who see it as tender, an act of loving service for those who see it as a serving love act, and a vicious, vengeful competition for those who see it as a vicious, vengeful competition. Life is the road to paradise for those who head towards it, and the road to hell for those who head towards it," I said with a smile.

She fell silent, so I continued:

"You see life through the lenses you have chosen for yourself. You create your thoughts, and then your thoughts create you. Life is not easy, nor is it difficult."

"How do I love?" she asked, confused.

"If I tell you, it will not help you, because whatever you do not practise will not benefit you. You must actually love to know what love is. There are things in life that one must achieve for oneself in order to be convinced of them, without being dissuaded by any creature," I said.

"How can a woman surrender her life to another who may not even be responsible for his own life?" she asked, confused.

"Because she will surrender herself into his hands at a time when her mind is working and her spirit is guiding her on the path of endless love, so that she may live in a security that no creature can give her, and she will grow with him and nurture him, and they will nurture each other on the path of life," I replied calmly.

She looked at me with that confused look and did not respond, so I said to her:

"If you are convinced by what I say, then know this: it is not enough to know these truths or to memorise them, you must practise them. What is the point of knowing all the keys to happiness without having the courage to open its doors and enjoy it?!"

We arrived then at the palace, and she looked at me with a mixture of confusion and love, anxiety and longing, calmness and excitement. Then she shook her head vigorously to shake off all the feelings that had overcome her.

"Leader, report on the losses," she shouted.

"Maid, take this man and bandage all his wounds, then carry out 111 with him," she shouted at the maid.

"We will continue our conversation after we have eliminated these barbarians," she said, looking at me with love.

The maid took me away, and I did not know what happened after that.

WHEN FANTASY PARTS WITH REALITY
NARRATED BY THE WOMAN, AGAIN

21- The Last War Against the Barbarians

An alert mind reached the peak of concentration, active eyes darting around, devouring everything in sight, sensitive ears detached from the world to compensate for what I could not see with my eyes, an attentive nose to compensate for the shortcomings of my ears, a clear mind, a bent back, There is a faint yellow smile that carries the meaning that I may die here and now, but it does not matter, I no longer care about that life. Perhaps this is the secret of the strength of the Amazons!

The horse runs on that line between the desert sand and the sky, riding on my horse, my upper teeth almost clasping my lower teeth from their feverish friction, my nose contracting and shrinking, my eyebrows narrowing and curving, my eyes flashing and thundering, and the horse continues on its way, and the line between the sand and the air has turned into a line between the water of the stream and the water of the sky, by which we mean the clouds.

Finally, I reached the battlefield where I saw my warriors lined up, ready to receive their orders and start the war.

Bare legs glisten in the darkness, expectant eyes devouring everything in sight, the left hand clutched the bow, and the right hand bent behind her back to take an arrow and pull it back smoothly, spears in the right hands and shields in the left.

I pointed the archers towards the sky, where the tree branches were.

"Method 516, we don't want anyone alive, use the serrated heads coated with rust and glue," I whispered to their leader.

Then I pointed to the hand-to-hand combatants at the cracks in the ground.

"Dip the blade in poison, leave no wounded alive, use technique 303," I whispered to their leader.

The rage boiling inside me could defeat the strongest and fiercest beasts. Their rage would not match mine, their fury would not match mine, and their excitement would not match mine. I looked proudly at my warriors.

When beauty reaches its peak, when physical strength reaches its limit, when emotional rigidity reaches its end, and when emotional stability reaches its ultimate extent, you have come somewhat close to the Amazonian way of life, the way that this man who violently invaded my life makes me question.

That war broke out, flared up quickly, then ended, and the earth was filled with dead bodies. We left no one alive, we did not discriminate, our revenge was terrible.

When I was done, I returned to the palace and ran to the old woman who had taught me about life.

"Bring the man here," I shouted to my maid, on the way I hurried to the old woman and rushed to her.

"You didn't tell me about this," I said as soon as I reached the old woman.

She turned to me.

"What is this thing I didn't tell you about?!" she asked me without surprise, for nothing could surprise that old woman after all she had seen.

The man arrived.

"This thing," I said.

22- Inquiry About The Meaning Of Life

To my great surprise, she understood immediately and shouted a shout conveying understanding.

"What do you want?!" she asked.

"I want to understand," I said in confusion as my tone was softened.

"You are more than just a woman to ask about such things. You are a queen, and not just any queen, you are the Queen of the Amazons. You are above such feelings," the old woman said calmly.

"What distinguishes me from my peers in this regard? My distinction should give me privilege, so that I can do what others cannot and what the incapable cannot do, not so that others can do what I am incapable of doing," I said in amazement.

"Do not take it as a privilege, but as a tax," the old woman said simply.

"Why should I pay that tax? To whom should I sacrifice?" I asked her in confusion.

"For your ideal society, the unique society we have created here, which is worth every sacrifice if there is a sacrifice needed to be made. We are the creators and the creation, the lyrics and the music. We have established our traditions and laws, and we ourselves apply them. We have shaped our lives to perfection with our own hands," she said.

Then the old woman pointed to the man.

"Look at them, they are all dogs chasing their desires, walking through life with no goal other than to satisfy their egos and prove themselves. We are superior to them, we are smarter than them, and we are also more skilled than them in all areas. They imposed their control only because they preceded us in imposing hegemony. The time has come to turn the tide and take control. We are here to lay the first brick with which we will rule the world," she continued.

"Not all of them," I said absent-mindedly.

"Most of them," she said emphatically.

"Marriage is not your way of life either. It is a weakness for an Amazon to depend on anyone, so she replaces family, home and stability with violence, bloodshed, brutality, destruction and war, and replaces love, contentment and satisfaction with hatred, greed and envy," she continued.

I looked around, feeling lost.

"Look at yourself, he's not right for you," the old woman continued, "no man will ever be right for you. You are higher and better than any man or woman. You are a being who combines brutality, strength, power and violence on the one hand, and tenderness, kindness and gentleness on the other. You are a unique being, a nun who is not suited to normal life. You are the queen. We crowned you queen because we could not make you more beautiful physically, or wiser mentally, or more stable emotionally, or more skilled and adept at fighting than you already are."

Then she pointed to my body.

"Anatomically, you are half male and half female," she added, "I left you one breast so that you would remember that you are female, and I removed the other so that you would remember that you are no longer female. Remember that you are a female but no longer just a female.

I looked at my body in confusion with mixed contradicting feelings of shame and pride.

"You have become above the genders of male and female. You do not have the foolishness of men and their animalistic lust, nor do you have the tenderness of women and their human compassion. You have become a beast without feelings. If someone calls for the female in your left half, let him see your right half," she said.

"I want the female in you to be male, and the male to be a beast," she added in a fervent enthusiastic tone.

Then she pointed to the man.

"Don't take appearances at face value, my dear. Anatomically, this is a male, but spiritually, the female is hidden inside him. Anatomically, you are female, but spiritually, a beast is hidden inside you," she concluded.

I looked at the man in confusion and thought, strange are these feelings that storm my heart, inside me is an overwhelming desire to throw myself at his feet like a wounded bird, sad and helpless, and inside me is also a fierce desire to protect him, embrace him, be kind to him and contain him.

All I want is to stay at his feet for the rest of my life.

"Those feelings are strong and overwhelming. They are not just instinct; they are something greater than that," I said to the old woman in confusion.

"I have told you what I can, and now you know everything and feel everything. You can think for yourself and make the decision that you see fit for you, but know one thing: you will never be queen again if you give in to those feelings," the old woman replied.

I was about to say something, but I felt that there was nothing more to say.

I took my beloved by the hand, gave a direct order to the leader, then carried him, placed him on the horse's saddle, and rode off with him.

23- THE MEETING THAT IS DESTINED TO BE THE LAST

The horse's hooves clicked on the green grass, and he galloped between the trees and rocks, jumping over the hills, circling around the slopes, splashing the water from the streams as he crossed them, his dark brown skin was painted by the red of the midday sun, his hooves drawing a poem on the grassy ground.

Finally, the horse stopped near the ocean shore. I dismounted and we walked along the beach, filled with confusion, not knowing what to do. Finally, he began to speak:

"I was certain that everything that happened to me had a purpose, but I didn't know what it was at the time. Only now do I understand."

I looked at him in confusion, and he continued:

"Life closed all its doors in my country, so I could board that ship that crashed to bring me here to you. Everything that happened in my life was to bring me to this moment, standing in front of you."

I was intoxicated by his words. Could words really have such an effect?

I looked at him lovingly as he continued:

"You don't need to do anything. Just be yourself, and your happiness, comfort and safety are my mission, which I will not compromise or neglect. Just be mine. Don't think, just be who you want to be. Be a queen and do what you do in your time. Just allow your heart to love and receive my love for you. Receive this free gift that asks nothing of you except to be yourself and enjoy your life."

His words made me happy, but despite myself, I said:

"Ask about me, man."

"Life has taught me not to ask someone whose mind differs from mine, so that his idea enters my mind. What use is his idea, which he formed with his mind, to my mind? Don't I deserve to think for myself and decide what is good for me?" he said stubbornly.

"You don't know how many I have killed, how many I have eaten, how many I have violated. I am different from you," I said somewhat shyly.

"And I accept you in this situation, and worse," he said insistently.

"See me as a little girl, waking up from sleep, her mother preparing her spear, sword, dagger, arrows and bow, ready to go to war, qualifying her to smash everyone's noses, to destroy everyone's pride, to provoke the enmity of everyone she meets, and to bring out the worst in them," I said somewhat painfully.

Then I continued sarcastically:

"See you as a little boy, waking up from sleep, his mother preparing sandwiches and schoolbooks for him, ready to go to school, qualifying him to heal the feelings of everyone who is sad, to forgive everyone who has wronged him, to bond lovingly with everyone he meets, and to bring out the best in him."

Then I continued regretfully:

"We are different. While your society rejoices at the birth of a boy and despises the birth of a girl, my society rejoices at the birth of a girl and discards the boy if he is born. I fought wars against savages when I was still young, and I learned to drink blood at a time when you were learning to cry out in your prayers, 'Save us from bloodshed, O God.' You do not need to draw attention to yourself, as your enormous self-confidence, which you derive from your morals, your kindness and your God, prevents you from begging people to give it to you, while I remain in need of trampling on people to gain that self-confidence, and I need to always remain at the top to feel confident."

"You were a crutch for your friend, helping him to be human, while I was a spear for my friend, stabbing her without hesitation or thought," I concluded.

"You don't know me, so how can you prejudge that we are not right for each other?!" he said stubbornly.

"The problem is not with us; the problem is with me alone. I am simply not fit to be anyone's lover," I said painfully.

"Nonsense, you will always be my lover, until death and beyond," he said confidently.

"I'm half woman, half man. Leave me alone. Can't you see I've given up half my chest?!" I said emotionally in defiance.

"I don't care about the anatomical half that's become more like a man. It's enough for me that you're internally a complete woman," he said sincerely.

"How can I be? I wasn't raised to be a woman, but to be a monster," I said frankly.

"You just have to open your heart, love everyone, then see what that behaviour leads to and observe it, and you will find the change easy after that," he said.

"Forget me, go back to your place and your country and forget me, forget that you ever saw me," I said in a tone dripping with sadness.

"I can't. I know this for sure. I won't forget you even if I try. I won't forget you even if I love someone else and get married. It's bigger than me, beyond my control," he said in a tone that brooked no argument.

"What do you want me to say?!" I said, confused.

"I don't know, just know that I loved you, I love you, and I will continue to love you," he replied, somewhat confused.

"Is there anything else?!" I asked him in a cold, frosty tone.

"If you respond to those feelings with such coldness, then there is truly nothing else," he said, pained by my coldness.

A group of female warriors arrived, and I pointed to them, to summon them.

"Take him to the neighbouring village, get him off that island to Island 440, and from there put him on any ship that will take him home. When you are sure he has boarded the ship, return here," I ordered.

They pulled him by his jacket and dragged him in front of them until they all disappeared from my sight, and for the first time in my life, a tear fell from my eye.

REALITY
NARRATED BY THE MAN, ONE LAST TIME

24- THE HOMELAND

Everyone died, everyone died. A piece of wood pierced his back, that boy drowned, this man's skull was broken, I slept, and then the next day I saw the wreckage of the ship that had anchored me here. I am on an island, and weeks have turned into months, and there is no ship, and I still do not see any sign of a ship, lying among the rocks, in the red water stained by my blood that flowed from the wounds caused by those rocks, my clothes are torn, my bones are broken, my skin is cracked. Finally, I pulled myself together and got up, feeling terrified and wondering: How bad is my situation?

Then I saw a war raging between savage men and women who were no less savage than them, a war between a snake and a snake, between a ferocious anaconda and a ferocious female snake.

I intervened, trying to save the woman who had disappeared into the anaconda's jaws. I stuck a tree branch into its mouth to prevent it from closing, and I disappeared inside its mouth. I grabbed the woman from inside and pulled her out.

Then I threw her safely to the ground, just as the snake closed in on me. I felt it pressing against my ribs, squeezing them to break them. I knew I screamed from inside its mouth:

"Oh God, accept my soul, I have no strength left. All I ask, my God, is to see her after my death. Please."

And I remembered, as I breathed my last breath inside the snake, my love for that queen.

Pain squeezes my inexperienced heart whenever I see you, woman, symbol of overwhelming beauty and excessive femininity, symbol of virility, strength and courage. What need do I have for a queen? It is torture to love a queen, not just a woman. She cast her net of love into my heart so that I would be affected by her and suffer for her. Perhaps for the first time, I taste pain, hitting the walls until they bleed.

And I remembered that I was dreaming. I am in a dream now, where reality and fantasy are mixed together. Of course, I saw the anaconda in a magazine and mixed it up with the rescue operation in which I saved my beloved, with the snake biting me inside it to swallow me, just as it happened to me when I loved her and she left me.

Perhaps it is time to wake up, so I will wake up. There is nothing to do here in this dream inside that snake.

I got up from my sleep and dragged myself to the bathroom. It was July, and the heat was unbearable. I stood barefoot on the bathroom tiles and looked at myself in the mirror: my hair was messy from lack of care, my back was bent from lack of happiness, my eyes were red from lack of sleep, and my features were sunken from lack of food. I had lost the will to live.

My mother literally lives for me. I don't mean that she lives to feed me, clothe me and take care of me, but I mean that my existence gives her the will to live and the strength to survive. It pains me to see her in that state. Sometimes I feel that her sadness for me exceeds my own sadness for myself.

Everyone around me loves me, so why don't you love me, my love? Is it my appearance, my face, my clothes, my behaviour, or my words that repel you? It would be difficult for me to change my behaviour and my words, and it is unnecessary for me to change my clothes. It is impossible for me to change my appearance and my face. Life is beautiful, all people are wonderful, the earth is flat, and we must treat bad people well to repair the break in our relationship. That is my principle. What has changed my principle so suddenly?

Some people create problems to experience sadness, revel in it, and bask in its fire. Some people create conflicts to experience anger. Some people live in tragedy to experience depression. Some people shut themselves in their rooms to experience loneliness. Some people who have plenty of time do this, but I do not.

What has now brought me into this terrible cycle of sadness that has no beginning and no end?

25- THE CAFÉ

"What can I get you, sir?" the waiter asked.

I turned to the waiter in alarm and moved away from him, raising my hand between us to ward off an imaginary threat he might pose to me, or fearing that he might slap me, hit me or insult me. My fear transferred to him, and he was afraid of me, imagining that I was mentally ill or something similar.

"A cup of coffee with extra sugar, please," I said, embarrassed.

"Right away," the waiter said eagerly.

He was pleased with the idea of getting away from me. I had indeed become a wreck after returning from that island. I became afraid of everything. I became terrified of the dark. Every hand raised high aroused my panic and anxiety. I became afraid of people and trembled in their presence.

I couldn't bear to look at them or face them, feeling that their gazes stripped me bare and exposed me, as if I were a hollow human being, empty of consciousness. I feared walls, I feared loneliness, I feared life, I was terrified of my own shadow, I was terrified of the idea of leaving my room, I hesitated before reaching out to shake someone's hand.

I have wasted a quarter of a century of my life thinking about principles and pursuing a life in the wrong direction. No wonder I was wrong from the start. Her rejection affected me as if I were a precious glass vessel filled with a rare and expensive liquid. That vessel fell, the liquid spilled, and the vessel shattered into a thousand pieces. I ended at the peak of my existence before I even began.

I shouldn't have loved her romantically. I should have just loved her humanly.

Sitting in that café with a cup of coffee in front of me, I think of a thousand thoughts, none of which I can pinpoint now. My schoolmate married some man, and I regret it in a way, even though I didn't want her. If she came to me now, I would accept her. The woman I loved left me, and it hurt me a lot, so why did I leave the one who loved me? I should have stayed with her. Maybe if I stayed with her, I would love her, just as if the woman I loved stayed with me and saw how much I loved her, she would love me. Maybe I would want to go back to my schoolmate as a kind of escape, or maybe it would be a kind of poetic justice in reverse, because I hope that the woman I loved who left me will come back to me, so I return to the one who loved me and I left her. I am on the verge of madness from thinking too much. I will waste my life thinking and planning without doing anything.

I got up to leave, and...

"The bill, sir," the waiter said, stopping me.

"What bill?!" I asked him in surprise.

He pointed to the coffee cup.

"The coffee bill," he said.

I glanced at the full cup and remembered it. I didn't have the energy or desire to drink it cold this time. I didn't sympathise with it. The cup had become aimless and purposeless. That was better. Let everything be aimless and purposeless. I have become aimless, so let everything else be that way too. This time, I will enjoy throwing it down the drain for nothing, but if it is aimless, why should I pay for it? Yes, yes, I too have a price, even if I live aimlessly, and so my price will be wasted and accounted for on the Day of Reckoning.

The man looked at me in surprise at my distraction, and I realised that I had to pay him his expenses. I would think about it later. I paid the man his money and wandered off, thinking that I had to recalculate everything from the beginning and rearrange my priorities.

You write a thousand letters, but you have no stamps, and there is no post box on the street. You make a thousand phone calls, and the answers vary between a busy signal and no answer. You walk around the room hundreds of miles, as if you are seeking something new, but there is nothing new. It is the same walls that witnessed your birth, the same ones that record your life, and perhaps the ones that will witness your death.

My pride prevented me from clinging to her when she told me to leave her. If only it hadn't prevented me! If only I had clung to her more! If only I hadn't left her!

Forget her? I cannot forget her. My back still bears the marks of the thorns that wounded me as I crawled to save it. Every mark reminds me of her. How can I forget her when her image is imprinted on my heart, my mind, and my skin? I breathe her in, I feel her presence all the time with a lump in my throat and a bitter taste in my mouth, because she is not really there.

It is beyond my tolerance, no one understands, no one appreciates, no one feels, it is just me, and hundreds of thoughts, thousands of aspirations and ambitions, and millions of feelings and emotions.

26- THE DAGGER

Sitting on my petrified sofa under the ceiling looming over my chest in the heart of my cold room covered in pitch darkness, I feel lonely, I feel desolate, I feel a frightening chill creeping down my spine and into my skull, my hands tremble from excessive hunger and thirst, my heart pounds between my ribs from excessive fear and terror, my legs shake from tension and anxiety.

Then it appeared suddenly!

It appeared in the heart of the darkness as if it had sprung from nowhere and dispelled the darkness.

It looked like a lamp.

I saw in its glow a beauty beyond description, I cannot describe her to you, all I can say is that she is a woman, yes, she is a woman in every sense of the word, I will not describe her features to you,

All I will tell you is that as soon as you see her, you will be certain that you have never before witnessed such tenderness, gentleness, calmness and beauty in one face. Her face appeared suddenly in the heart of the darkness in the light of that faint glow. Wait, that thing that glowed in the darkness was nothing but a long dagger. She moved towards me with slow steps, then stopped two steps away, brandished the dagger in my face and waved it, but I did not care. She saw the admiration in my eyes and did not care, plunging it into my heart up to the hilt, then walked away coldly. I tried to move in the dark, stumbled, fell, cried, felt weak, felt helpless, felt oppressed, and my pain and failure multiplied. I had never felt such pain before.

Finally, I managed to get out of my room and ran to my family, silent and in pain. I did not ask any of my family members to remove the dagger, and they did not see it. I gritted my teeth in pain, and they did not feel what I was suffering. They even asked me to do trivial unimportant tasks, which aroused my anger and rage. I rebelled against them and left the house.

The strangers on the street made me feel even more alone than I did in my cold, dark room. That boy with that girl, that young man with that young woman, that dude with that chick. I was alone with a dagger dripping with blood, a trail of my blood following me from my room to the street, and no one noticed me.

Ah, ah, ah, ah.

Finally, I reached my friends. They also did not see the dagger. I told them about it, and they noticed it. One of them tried to pull it out quickly and forcefully. It hurt, and when the dagger did not come out, I screamed and cried out in pain. I begged that friend to leave it alone, but he said no. He continued his attempts until he pulled it out. My blood gushed out, and he tried in vain to stop the bleeding, but it did not stop.

My friends took me on a trip to the amusement park, and the bleeding continued. We ran, played football, and had fun, but the bleeding continued. We sat, slept, stood, and walked, but the bleeding continued.

After some time, the wound began to heal. I looked at the dagger lying on the ground, picked it up, and opened the wound as it was. I began to live with it. My friends passed by, and when they saw the wound and how bad it had become, they were surprised and asked what had happened. When I answered them, they became angry with me and left me, saying, "How weak you are!" I lost their respect and their commitment to me.

A beautiful girl passed by, holding a fragrant flower in her hand, which seemed to have the ability to heal that wound, but I enjoyed seeing the image of the woman I loved on the tip of the dagger she stabbed me with. The beautiful girl left me, saying, "One day you will regret leaving me like this for no reason, without us ever meeting."

"My beloved also left me for no reason and without meeting me," I cried out on the inside in amazement.

"Why doesn't the one I love love me, and why does the one I don't love love me? Why does this curse continue through the generations without a cure?" I cried out internally.

I will find a cure for it.

Years later.

I removed the dagger, and the wound healed, leaving a deep scar that even time could not erase. I live with it now and have adapted to it.

I no longer wish for my beloved to return, and time has taught me not to enjoy the memory of her leaving me. I only wish that something unknown would happen in my life to change that painful reality.

27- THE POTTERY

I had to go to him, that wise old man whom I know well, who has always guided me when I was lost on the paths of life, confused in my choices of destinies, and tests of fates. It is certain that life repeats itself but with different faces, so the events that happen to you have happened to those before you, so why not benefit from the experiences of those who came before you?

In the end, when I failed to deal with those feelings on my own, and when the wheel of loss trampled me, I went to him with all the information and my wounded feelings. As usual, the answer seemed as clear as day to him, while it remained hidden from me, perhaps because of his wisdom, or because I am immersed in my story to the core, or perhaps because it is difficult to give advice to oneself, or because it is difficult to implement.

The question that raced through my mind and burned in my brain was whether there was a purpose behind all this. And if there was a purpose, what was it?

"Yes, there was a purpose. The purpose was to reform that woman, and when that woman is reformed, the tribe she leads will be reformed with her. You were sent to her to benefit her. You planted a seed in that woman's soil, and you should not have left parts of your soul in the mud of her land. You have affected her in some way, and her life will never be the same after you," he said.

This was the wise man's answer, which brought me back to my senses. I thought about what he said and found it to be frighteningly true. I had failed when I let my feelings slip out of control. I should not have let my emotions run wild, rage, and revolute without the slightest control from my mind.

"But what about me? Did I make a mistake when I loved her? Or was my love for her part of the plan? Why did I have to be broken? What did I gain from it?" I said in pain.

"You had to be broken in order to become stronger. You had to melt in the flames to become soft dough, so that you could be moulded into something stronger, better shaped and purer. The only way to shape you is with fire. That is how you grow. Because your metal is good and your essence is strong, it was necessary for you to be broken greatly, so that the impurity nestled deep within you could be purified," he said calmly.

He paused for a moment, then continued:

"That flaw may be waiting for praise from people and watching people's reactions to your actions. Although this does not seem apparent on the outside, in a way you were doing the right thing not for God but for the glorification and veneration of yourself. Therefore, when you did not get the expected reaction, you rebelled and raged, but only inside yourself. That hidden internal blow was what destroyed your mind, upset your balance, and destroyed your self-confidence."

He gestured with his hand and continued:

"It wasn't just her rejection that destroyed your self-confidence. Her excessive self-confidence shattered all the pride you had in yourself. It became a battle between her self-confidence and yours. and she defeated you with her boundless self-confidence, trapping you in a terrible vicious circle, a bottomless pit called loss of self-confidence, when she rejected you in that way."

He pressed on my wound with extreme violence.

"Everything you say is true, but you haven't given me the solution. I'm in pain, really in pain!" I said in pain.

"We all have to experience pain. Some people suffer unnecessarily for the rest of their lives and remain in a state of misery. Sometimes these people come to enjoy the pain. Others are driven by pain to reform themselves, refine their character and improve their behaviour. Pain is a path that all human beings must walk, and they may use it for their benefit or to their detriment, but the most severe type of pain is the first type, as it leads to no purpose, but rather to more and more pain," he said calmly.

He pointed his finger tenderly and continued:

"You can dwell and wallow in pain, or you can start living before life ends. Don't be one of the first kind, my friend. Use pain to improve yourself, to rise in rank, and to grow in character. You don't know how much that woman hurt you and to what extent she did it. Where did those words about the blue diamond and the red pearl go? Where did all your principles go? Where did your gratitude for everything all the time go, and your belief that everything that happens to you is somehow for your own good? Where did your old way of thinking go? What good are all those principles you hold dear if you don't use them when you need them?!"

I thought deeply, but couldn't find the right answer to that question, so I shrugged my shoulders in confusion and said:

"I don't know."

Then, as if he had been waiting for my confusion, he said:

"You loved your opposite just because she was your opposite. You loved her rebellious beauty, her deadly strength, her powerful personality and her formidable presence. And because you loved her so deeply, your emotions unconsciously embraced her principles in solidarity with her and in unity with his being. When she left you and moved on, you felt a terrible crack in your being, a crack in your aching, wounded affection that arose from the pain of loneliness and the agony of separation, and a crack in your principles that fractured when her thoughts invaded them and collapsed when she left you after leaving parts of her soul in your being. Those parts made you feel lonely and confused your thoughts, so you became willing to do what you wanted and what she wanted, to love and to hate, to reconcile and to fight, to be humble and to be arrogant."

He clapped his hands gently, perhaps to get my attention, and continued:

"And that terrible war raged inside you without you knowing, so you said: I may be wrong in everything I have thought and in all the principles on which I have built my life, and perhaps for the first time you have split yourself apart, so you have come to hate yourself for two reasons, the first for her rejection to you and the second for her wrong path. Your pain is too difficult to describe and too great to bear."

My emotions were clearly visible on my face. He was sincere, sincere to the utmost degree, more than anyone could imagine. And so he knocked on hot iron and continued:

"My friend, let go of the impurities she left in your mind and heart. Erase her existence from your life. Love another, and deep, mutual, lasting love will make you forget every other memory. Start a new path with a new spirit, now that you are wiser and stronger than before. Do not compromise your fundamental principles. Everything that happened was a terrible test of all your convictions and the strength of their foundation."

"And did I fail the test?!" I said regretfully.

"You will now decide whether you have succeeded or failed. Will you give in to feelings of despair, loss, loneliness and desolation, or will you come out of your room and your solitude and start facing life again, stronger than before, with that experience having left you with valuable lessons? Will you be grateful for having gone through it, since you would not have experienced all this if you had not gone through that experience?!" he said, instilling more hope and dispelling the pain.

I remained silent, wanting to act, not to speak. I thanked him and left without wasting words on promises and vows. I will do the right thing now, and I will not delay for a second.

Now that I had the answer, I knew that I had left the one who loved me, and the one I loved had left me. I understood that the goal was not love itself, but to remain forever in a state of mutual love.

What good is my knowledge if the pit is fallen into by those who know and those who do not know? I will work on myself to benefit from that experience.

My love, you should not have let the opportunity for love pass you by like that. No one deserves to live their whole life alone. It does not benefit anyone to make such a pointless sacrifice against themselves. Forgive me, my dear, for despite your exceptional qualities, which I acknowledge and admit, you are, in the end, just one woman among all these women.

I have my whole life ahead of me to live, a long life to enjoy, and many people around me.

Why should I imprison myself within walls, waste my time, and limit my world to just two girls?

And so I raised my head, took a deep breath, and decided to face life in a new way, to wait for that new creature whom I will love and who will love me.

We are back to the beginning again. Everything that happened had a purpose, and I think I know what it is now.

— — —

Cairo, February 2009

NOVEL III
DAGGER

*For those who carry their wounds in silence.
May these pages work as a reminder that
pain does not end the story,
and that even the darkest paths can lead to
healing and redemption.*

CHAPTER ONE
THE DAGGER

I gazed tenderly at my three-year-old child, studying his small, carefully formed features. I knew these hours when he drifts to sleep were the only moments free of mischief, noise, crying, or wailing. I smiled as I watched him, a reflex, and my mind wandered.

The most beautiful moments in a man's life are those when he witnesses the birth of his first son: his continuation in the world, his hope for a better tomorrow, his desire that his son accomplish what he himself could not. A creature born of his love for the most beautiful being in his eyes: his wife.

Yet I am leaving this hope behind in a society whose education system teaches nothing; a land too cramped to give its people shelter or work, where goods and services cost the earth. Its people either feast on honey or go hungry; they walk the crowded streets with faces heavy with gloom, unable to tolerate even a touch without exploding. Morality has decayed; bribery is accepted as a given. Falsehood is sanctified with the excuse that everyone does it, and that they are simply recovering what was taken from them, despite them. Security violates every right in this poor nation; order has turned to chaos and chaos to slaughter. The government is like a tourist from another country, asleep and oblivious, like an alien body from another planet, its rulers like occupiers. The poor are a sharp, rusted, poisonous sword; the rich are a soft, swollen mass of dough. The merchants beg, steal, plunder, and take bribes. The young grind their teeth with suppressed anger, gnawing at whatever flesh of their women appears. The intellectuals collapse under diabetes, high blood pressure, heart disease — and, at minimum, chronic depression. The children are left disabled by the horrors they have seen, the ugliness they have heard, the filth they have touched.

I am neither a political analyst nor a social investigator nor an economist to explain why things are so. I only observe what happens around me without certain knowledge of the causes that brought us to this point. This time I regarded my son with different eyes.

What world am I leaving him in? How long will he remain innocent in this rotten world? How long will he keep his morals in that corrupt realm? How can I ask him to beware of colleagues who will envy him, coworkers who will entrap him, subordinates who will flatter him, bosses who will grind him, relatives who will forget him in the grind for a crust of bread, a lover who will never know the taste of love with; after all the failures and sorrows he will endure, and his own self which will work against him after being crushed by such psychological wounds?

Against my will, I found myself going to the dagger. I do not remember exactly when or how I got it. Was it from that new friend, the Buddhist monk? From the National Museum?

From that unexplored cave of unknown location, I once visited? From the shop opposite my workplace? Truly, I cannot recall how I acquired this dagger. I only remember that it is valuable, that no one must ever know of it, and that it belongs to me alone.

I held it and studied it closely. Its handle was set with red rubies and white gold; diamonds and gems formed a beautiful pattern. The blade was sharp and gleaming, its hue leaning toward volcanic red — neither heavy nor light.

I went to the child, and all the dark thoughts swirled through my head. Finally, I thought: if I suffer all this suffering, I will not allow him to become an extension of my pain. Farewell, my little one.

I slit his throat quietly.

Afterward... I wiped the clotted blood from his neck, told his mother he died in his sleep, shed a few tears, then buried him — with the dagger — in the earth, as he was before we brought him to this world. It was certainly better for him.

— † —

That dog means everything to me now, after the carnival of people around me dispersed: colleagues, friends, relatives, family, father and mother, brothers and sisters, wife and children. Everyone has gone — to their doom, to isolation, to busyness — and they all shared one act: they left me alone.

I want nothing from life. It has taught me, in instalments, that it will take me piece by piece: my teeth after my hair, my bowed head, the decay of some of my organs; my ear, my eye, and the wasting of others; my limbs, my chest.

Wait! My dog runs toward that muddy patch in the park and drags me with violent force. It begins to dig in the earth, turning the mud upside down. At last, it pulls its mouth from the hole with a dagger; silver with a red sheen, a magnificent blade and handle, and drops it into my trembling hands.

I grasped the dagger; it trembled in my grip with excitement. I gazed at it in wonder. Surely this blade could make me rich if I sold it; yet money is of little value to someone like me. Something made me tuck it into my pocket, and I walked away calmly while the agitation simmered inside me.

Revenge; vengeance for the man who killed my father. I knew my father had been murdered; I did not know, nor did anyone, who killed him. My memory, which was fading, began to stir, much to my amazement. I see my father and the father of the man whose son — also three years old — died, working together. That man, a close friend of my father, my father caught skimming money from the company's accounts. The other man threw him from a height onto the ground; his skull shattered, his blood mixed with flesh and bone on the asphalt, then slid into the cracks toward the mud; the very mud that yielded the dagger. It seems the dagger awakens deep suppressed memories. My father's blood screamed at me through the blade.

So, my feet carried me to the café where the son of the man who killed my father sat. When I saw him, I whispered a few words in his ear and left. I waited in the dark alley. When he came out, the dagger plunged into his belly and withdrew again, then sank into him elsewhere, and left it to meet it to again part with it, until it had made ten openings in his belly. Finally, I removed it and left, satisfied.

At last, I had avenged my murdered father. The dagger had served me well; it told me who killed my father, helped me kill him, and gave me the courage to go through with the act. But in the end, I had to get rid of it. I walked to the Eastern Riverbank and dropped it without anyone noticing into the deep waters, letting it sink like a jewel through the cosmic void among the fish. I returned home calmly, certain I would escape my crime, which I'm proud of. Who would suspect an old man with arthritis, trembling nerves, and a selected set of modern ailments?

— † —

I had to take the ferry home, which would take far longer because I had no bus fare, not a penny in my pocket. Slowly, over the quiet moving water of the Eastern Riverbank, I glimpsed the dagger's blade glittering, stuck in a big fish. Perhaps someone had caught the fish and forgotten to retrieve the weapon, or the rope that bound it had come loose.

I ran to the ferryman and begged him for a scoop net. I grabbed it, ran to the fish with the blade lodged in it, and hauled both out with a swift pull. I eased the fish off the blade but failed at first; I tried harder and succeeded. I admired the gleaming weapon in astonishment and forgot everything about the fish. That blade must be worth a fortune, wealth, wealth.

Why must I live in the torment of poverty when I could live in plenty until I die? That plenty lies with my rich old uncle. Of course, my wealthy uncle has many heirs among whom the inheritance will be scattered; I, the poor pauper of the family, will find myself equal to the wealthy branch. Justice, due to this weird situation, would become injustice; thus, inverting the scale of justice, as I think, can be tipped through flipping the cards, and providing relief to an old man from his misery, grief, pain, and loneliness. My mind calmed and the solution — obvious to me for a long time — shone as a perfect one for everyone.

The ferry arrived. I handed the scoop net and the big fish to its keeper, whose face lit with a pleased smile, and I hid the dagger in my boot and ran light-footed to where the house is, my uncle's house, not my house. I knocked. No one answered at once; I steadied my nerves and waited. Finally, the door opened and my uncle appeared, greeting me warmly:

"My dear, my beloved nephew. How I missed you!"

He embraced me tenderly; I returned his hug treacherously. I drew the dagger from my boot while he patted my shoulder in fatherly concern. I plunged the blade into his back; it sank through bone and flesh and burst his weak, diseased heart, releasing a volcanic flood of blood. The tip of the dagger protruded from his chest and grazed my chest.

I dropped my uncle's body, went into the flat, looted the gold, money, and valuables, wrapped his corpse with the dagger still embedded with bedsheets, and carried him to the neighbourhood bakery. I paid my friend the baker to cremate his body in the big oven in the back, leaving the dagger to burn with him, and I returned home calmly.

— † —

I put tomatoes and courgettes in the same bag and walked to the bakery for bread. I bought twenty loaves, returned home, put everything in the kitchen, and started cooking for my crippled mother, my low-income father, and my seven siblings. I took the tomatoes and courgettes from the bag and found that a courgette had pierced a soft tomato. I was angry, knowing the damage could not be undone, and my thoughts flew to my lover, my companion who loved me and whom I loved; the poor man who couldn't earn to buy his daily bread. Once, with a look of aching desire, he devoured me with his gaze, and in a lapse of both our minds he acted. I became pregnant; my shame haunted me wherever I went, like a fetus within me.

I took out a loaf so it wouldn't stick to the others, moving each away from its neighbour. My thoughts devoured me. I was not angry that he had done it; I wanted him too. I did not care that he was poor; I too was poor. What made me furious was his refusal to admit what he'd done, especially after the fortune that had landed in his lap. Wait — that loaf feels heavier than it should. I opened it cautiously, afraid of what might spring at me, but nothing moved inside. A dagger lay between the slices. I gripped it in agitation; the fluorescent light flashed on its blade and planted in my mind the meaning of washing shame. "Wash your shame! Wash your shame! He cannot be anyone's if he is not yours, and he should not be a father for a child if it's not your child! Kill him! Kill him!"

Murder took on a meaning, purification from sullied love, release from baseness, cowardice, and escape from responsibility. In a fit of rage, I plunged the dagger into the courgette that had crushed and caused the tomato to bleed everywhere. I realised the purpose behind obtaining that dagger; to take vengeance on the one who stained me, to strip my wrapping away without flinching.

I did not wait. I leapt into my shoes, ran down the stairs of our house, climbed the stairs to his, and knocked. He peered through the peephole and opened the door eagerly. He took me in his blazing arms with instinctual hunger; I consented to one last embrace. I led him like a mule to the bed, threw myself upon him with feigned affection.

"Close your eyes," I said gently.

He did so silently. I drew the dagger quietly, with murderous cold and great composure, then leapt, plunging it into his chest right over his heart so the polluted heart would spew blood, that is more on the black side than it is red. No one would suspect me; we had never been seen together. I would escape blame; I knew it with certainty. I left the dagger buried in his heart and walked away as I had come, simply and calmly, as if returning from a morning walk.

— † —

What right had her to steal the man I loved? She is no better than I. Why should she enjoy him and I not? What sets her apart from me? She is me and I am her, the same beauty, the same figure, the same poverty, the same illiteracy, the same strength, the same oppression. Why did she take him and charm him until she bore his child? She knew I loved him first, though she did not love him; she nevertheless chose to steal him, taking pleasure in seeing the one who loved her without loving him in return, in a deliberate humiliation of his emotions; as she intentionally meant to conquer me, as she watched my heart getting devoured by pain, enjoying the scene in pure savage pleasure.

And here is my beloved, murdered on his bed, and the public prosecutor's men classify the case as unknown perpetrator as he had no enemies. The forensic technician, whom my meagre bribe could feed his family for a week, brings me the murder weapon; the dagger that had lodged in my beloved's heart. I hold it, looking at it with grief as my mind returns with the face of my loved one who died with his eyes closed.

He died loving her. He was alive for her and will forever be hers. She has robbed me of the reality of existing with him, of the phantom of feeling of his spirit hovering around me which surely hovers around her. No, I will not allow his ghost to circle her; I will send it back to him, so they burn together in hell, slowly, piece by piece. Let their ghosts haunt me if they dare.

The gnawing, murderous jealousy in my gut will never leave me as long as she lives. One of us must die. I hid the dagger in the folds of my embroidered, brightly coloured dress and went to the tailor's where she works. I waited in the restroom. When she entered the last stall, I knew she would use, and before she could close the door when she saw me, I wedged the dagger as a blockade. Before she could scream, I stuffed a piece of the shop cloth into her mouth and plunged the dagger into her neck up to the hilt, then with a simple twist removed her head. I watched her bleed to fill my eyes with the sight of her getting her due.

At last, I threw the dagger into the drain and flushed; the water swallowed it instinctively, and it vanished completely. Again, a perfect crime.

— † —

Some kill when they collapse; the thin thread separating conscious intent from unconsciousness snaps, when reason is swept in a fit of madness, and genius becomes folly, so they kill in a state of imbalance. Some kill for betrayal, some take revenge for a murdered loved one, or to avenge the outrage to one of their women; some kill for greed, or driven by jealousy, or as the final act of a lifelong suppressed rage. I am none of these. I kill for the sake of killing; a kind of madness in which the afflicted believes himself the sanest of men. I treat death as the one absolute truth in this world of illusions. Everything around us moves toward some place at some time. I accelerate that timing; I am an auxiliary force of the universe, an enhancing catalyst. Discovery of my crimes is impossible, a path of fantasy. My killings have no specific motive, no distinguishing trait, and no characteristic weapon.

Anything may lead to anything. Logic of the illogical, the random road. I kill anyone, anywhere, anytime, by any method, with any weapon. My life itself is atypical: I live anywhere, take any job, eat anything. I am the embodiment of randomness.

Tonight, I decided to leave the lair I occupy and slit the throat of the first man or woman I see on the street with that dagger that came down from the sewer above my head and take whatever they have to eat for my supper. I went out and found a girl wearing an embroidered, brightly coloured dress.

I moved toward her as though I did not; so, she did not flinch or flee; she only gasped when the dagger drew a red line under her breast, a long horizontal wound that threw some of her entrails into the street.

I whistled with pleasure as I emptied her pockets, then left the place happy, hurling the dagger with full strength so it smashed through the glass of a window.

— † —

"Study, study, study! any word that might help you. Don't walk barefoot on the cold tiles. Close the fridge well. Don't drink cold water lest you catch a cold before exams. Turn off the television; it won't help. Come spit on my grave if you succeed. Don't bring your eyes that close to the TV."

"I am human; I cannot bear all these orders and prohibitions without a single encouraging word, without one touch of care, without one orphaned pat on my shoulder."

"…!"

"Enough! Enough! Enough!"

"Are you shouting at me, you cursed little thing? Dare you answer me? How dare you raise your voice at me, you failure?!"

"I will raise my voice. I will raise it!"

"I will tell everyone your truth; so, they know you are not the innocent angel you pretend to be, but a filthy devil."

"What is all this evil? Does a mother speak to her only son like this?!"

"You are a wicked son unworthy of life. I wish I had miscarried and not bore you."

"All this for studying?!"

"All this because you disappointed me, because I wasted my life on you. I wish I had not had you! We would have been rid of you."

Glass shattered. The dagger flew across the room and fell into the hand of the boy, who looked at his mother with indescribable anger. He flung the dagger from his grip, and it spun, the blade settling in his hand and then he threw it arcing toward his mother's chest. It pierced her.

The cold metal of the blade mingled with the bones of his mother who had given him his sturdiness, with her blood that ran in his veins, with the sweat she shed preparing his food and comfort, with the flesh that wore from standing long hours in the kitchen for his sake, with the milk that nourished him.

For a moment the boy looked at her, then ran to her, crying in grief, screaming:

"What have you done?!"

He cried and cried. All this because of anger, all because of anger. He pulled the dagger out and hurled it out the window in fury and revolt.

— † —

The dagger flew through the air. It knows it will find its way to pierce the chest of the boy struck by it. That is its law: it kills by the hand that kills with it; so, the circle of killing continues without end and the flood of blood that covers the world after Cain killed his brother rolls on.

The tale of blood will have no beginning and no end unless someone stops the flood with the dam of love, love that gives consolation to the miserable who lost his son, that plants forgiveness in the heart of the avenger, that brings relief to the uncle who killed, contentment to the nephew who murdered his kin for money, chastity and innocence to the one misled by lust who erred, vengeance to the one blinded by honour who kills like the girl who murdered the one she loved, comfort and peace to the one driven to kill for killing's sake, and patience and mercy to the enraged.

The reader holding this story became a killer when the dagger fell into their hand. Why did you do it, you miserable person? You cannot deceive the dagger! It will find its way to you.

CHAPTER TWO
HATRED MANIFESTATION

"What is this? Are you experimenting on me?" I turned sharply toward the doctor holding the syringe, with panic in my voice.

"What's that?" I cried again, eyes fixed on the needle aimed at my vein.

"Keep that thing away from me!"

But he didn't care. He pressed the syringe in until the last drop was gone, then walked out silently.

"No!" I screamed in terror.

Suddenly, I rose from the bed, weightless. I was no longer bound by gravity. I kept ascending until my back hit the ceiling. I tried to pull myself free but couldn't. Slowly, I began to flatten, turning into a paper-thin sheet, my being spilling out of my body in a cascade of light and...

"Wake up. Wake up. It's just a dream."

Who said that? It was me. It had to be me. I live alone.

My family is with their Creator. My two children live with my ex-wife. My fiancée — my beloved — still lives with her parents. My brothers are abroad.

It's only me here. Just me.

I reached for the pistol beside me; seeking the false comfort it gave, something I never truly had. I threw the covers aside and stood up. I pressed the answering machine button and listened to the messages on my way to the bathroom.

"You have three new messages."

I squeezed toothpaste onto the brush.

"David, it's me. I called to tell you that we have to end this. I told you many times before, but you never listened. I didn't want to weaken again in front of you, so I'm leaving this message instead; so, you can hear it once, twice, even three times until you actually believe me.

Your life is far too complicated for me. Children, an ex-wife, one fugitive brother, another in prison..."

Ah, yes... the brother in prison. I had almost forgotten him. And who was she to call the one abroad a fugitive?

I spat the foam and fragments of toothpaste into the sink as her voice went on:

"Secret missions, sudden assignments, orders and travel; it's all too much. You are too much for me, David. You don't even know yourself or what you want. You're lost, and you'll drag me down with you. I can't say I know what I want, but I know clearly what I don't want. You. Forgive me, and don't try to call again. Goodbye."

I walked out of the bathroom and stared at the packet of seized drugs on the table, hesitating. Inside my mind, voices clashed — some urging, some forbidding. Then I thought of my deserting lover, of my ex-wife, of my broken life.

I lit the roll, mixing in a strange new blend of narcotics, and pressed the next message.

"David, bad news, man. All the stocks have dropped, and I don't think they'll rise again. I told you not to put all your savings in that cursed company. Sell now. Save what you can—fast. Now."

My teeth clenched hard. In frustration and hesitation, I pressed the third button.

"Good morning, David. Go immediately to the address I sent you on your phone. It's an urgent case."

I showered again and took a couple of stimulants. I'd need every shred of focus for this urgent case.

Who was it that once said a man should separate his personal life from his work? I wished he were here to give me advice now.

— † —

"Good morning, Major Sam," I said.

That's how I greeted Major Sam—my superior and my friend at once.

"Good morning, Detective David. Please, sit." He replied absently, gesturing for me to sit.

I sat, watching him carefully. He looked tense, anxious in a way I'd never seen before. He exhaled sharply, releasing his unease.

"What do we have, David?" he asked.

I placed a photo before him, an older man in his late forties, sitting behind an enormous desk, a strange, elegant dagger buried deep in his chest.

"The victim," I said, "a well-known fiction writer, forty-four years old, unmarried. Died from a stab wound straight to the heart. The dagger remained lodged in place, as you see."

Sam intertwined his fingers on the desk.

"And who benefits from his death?" he asked.

I shook my head.

"No one," I said. "The man practically knew no one. Lived alone. Worked alone. Lived off his writing. No lover, no children, no friends. His relatives are either dead or abroad. He truly knew no one."

Sam looked stunned for a moment.

"So, someone knew that. Knew he lived alone. Decided to rob him. He surprised the intruder, and the killer had to silence him," Sam said.

I shook my head again.

"Look at these," I said, laying out photos of the study where the murder took place.

The photos showed a vast study; three walls lined from floor to ceiling with towering bookshelves crammed with thousands of volumes. Every inch was filled with books except where three windows, one window per wall, framed carefully so the shelves wouldn't block them. The door was set in the middle of the fourth wall. In the horseshoe-shaped space at the centre stood a massive, stately desk facing the door. On the bare wall hung a PhD certificate in literature bearing the author's name, flanked by two paintings: a sunset to the left, a sunrise to the right, and between them a long canvas of a waterfall cascading beneath a clear blue sky.

To the left of the door was a sofa with a small table in front of it and a mini fridge beside it; evidence the writer ate in his study often.

"As you can see," I explained, "no signs of forced entry. As for the rest of the apartment — bathroom, kitchen, living room, and bedroom, it's as if no one lived there. You'll see for yourself; the place looks like a display unit in a showroom."

I showed him more photos.

"In short, nothing was stolen. His modest savings are untouched," I said.

"Then how was the murder discovered?" Sam frowned.

"Her. She heard the victim scream and called the police." I pointed to a photo of a young maid.

Sam rested his chin on his clasped fists, elbows on the desk.

"There's a mystery here, David," he said. Then, almost to himself, "The motive."

"There's a greater mystery than that." I smiled faintly.

He looked up.

"The method," I said mysteriously.

"What do you mean?" he asked curiously.

"When the police arrived, the door was locked from the inside." I said, pointing at the photos again.

"The room was sealed. The three windows were closed from the inside and fitted with metal bars, impossible to pass through. The only door was locked from within—no forced entry anywhere. There's no way the killer could've left after committing the murder. Everything was sealed shut."

Sam was silent for a long moment. Then, with sudden triumph:

"He killed himself. There's no other explanation."

"No," I said calmly. "He didn't. The dagger had no fingerprints—none. His hands were bare, no gloves. There was nothing in the room he could've used to wipe the handle. And his face... it didn't look like that of a man who chose to die. Besides, stabbing oneself with a dagger is a strange way to commit suicide."

"Did the forensics report add anything?" he asked hopefully.

"Nothing. No prints in the room but his," I said, shaking my head.

He frowned.

"Isn't it odd the dagger had no prints at all? I'm telling you; he killed himself," Sam said.

"I don't know," I said, lost in thought. "But I can't understand how someone's own hand could obey an order to end his life."

"Psychological stress," he replied quickly. "He was lonely—desperately lonely. He had a moment of weakness he couldn't endure and gave in."

"And wiped his fingerprints how?" I pressed.

He sighed. "Let's go over this again. We have a victim with a dagger in his chest. Not suicide, no prints, no gloves, no intrusion. No motive for theft, no close acquaintances, no one to suspect. Did he really know no one his entire life?" Sam asked.

I pointed to a stack of papers from the victim's desk. "Only his writings. I'll read them at home—maybe they'll tell us something."

"That's... tragic." Sam shook his head sadly.

"It seems so." I nodded.

He stared off, distracted. "You seem troubled." I said softly.

He twirled his mustache. "It's a strange case," he said, thinking deeply.

"Don't worry. We'll catch the killer, like always." I smiled reassuringly.

"And what exactly will you do in this case, David?" he frowned, thoughtful.

"I'll solve its riddle. I knew it was an impossible case, because they sent it to our division. It probably baffled both the police and the prosecution." I shrugged lightly.

A wave of dizziness hit me. "We'll solve it," I murmured. "I just need to do a bit of thinking, and a lot of fresh air. If you'll excuse me."

I left his office, my mind circling endlessly around the case as I drove home. Thoughts of my lover's rejection, my lost money, and the drug coursing through my veins tangled inside me. My body felt heavy, my head light. Somehow, I reached home without remembering the road. I collapsed onto my bed, drained to the last nerve, surrendering to sleep, thus ending another day in this weary life.

CHAPTER THREE
THE IMPOSSIBLE INVESTIGATION

"Sir, I've never worked on a case like this before," I told Major Sam the moment I entered his office early the next morning. He looked at me with surprise.

"What do you mean? Take responsibility, man. Who else should I assign this case to, if not you?" he asked.

I raised my hands defensively.

"Sir, no! God forbids! I'm not trying to step away. I just need help."

"Help from whom?" he frowned.

"Anyone who understands supernatural matters," I answered quickly. "The case has no suspects, no fingerprints, no enemies, no way of escape. I'm stuck. It's the first time I've faced something like this."

Sam spoke gently, as if trying to plant peace and quietness inside me.

"Don't worry, my friend."

He patted my hand, then placed three files in front of me.

"These belong to three of the finest people who ever handled cases like this, at least, to my knowledge."

I began reading aloud:

"Agent Fox Mulder, X-files, FBI Special Agent. Olivia Dunham, Fringe Division, FBI Special Agent. Refaat Ismail... medical doctor."

I paused in surprise. "Who's Refaat Ismail?"

"He's an Egyptian haematologist," explained Sam calmly. "He happened to encounter many supernatural events throughout his life."

"Can they come with me to the crime scene?" I asked sceptically.

He smiled. "Of course. We've already signed coordination protocols between our departments. No problem. Naturally, we'll owe them a favour in return."

I nodded quickly. "Of course... of course."

— † —

Olivia Dunham burst into the room with her classic breach-and-clear style, gun drawn.

Behind her strode the tall, composed Fox Mulder, flashing his badge and declaring solemnly, "FBI."

Refaat Ismail slipped under Mulder's raised arm, dodging Olivia's outstretched pistol, and entered shouting irritably.

"What do you expect to find here? The man is already dead!" Refaat murmured in anger.

"It's protocol," Mulder replied abrasively.

"Caution never hurts. Recklessness does," Olivia added without looking at him.

Mulder hurried towards a sword hanging on the wall beside the door, examining it in fascination. Olivia flipped through a photo album on the desk. Meanwhile, Refaat leaned over the corpse, gently lifting the victim's eyelids and shining a faint light into the pupils.

"Time out!" I snapped my fingers sharply. They all turned towards me.

"What are you doing?" I asked.

In unison, they replied, "working."

"Working?" I shouted, "By staring at a sword and flipping through family photos?"

"Please, don't interfere with my work. Don't forget; you asked for our help." Mulder's voice came back rough and steady.

I nodded, half-apologetic, and turned to study the books lining the shelves. Olivia examined the desk drawers, while Refaat continued inspecting the body.

Mulder looked out through the barred window and muttered, "I'll need Agent Scully."

"Apologies," I said politely, "but the best I could do was bringing you."

Olivia finished checking the desk and straightened up.

"We'll need Dr. Walter to perform the autopsy," Olivia said.

"I'm afraid Dr. Walter can't be here," I said. "You'll have to work with Dr. Ismail."

Olivia eyed Refaat's bald head and frail frame suspiciously before asking, "can you handle this autopsy, Dr. Ismail?"

"Of course, Agent Dunham." He snorted, spat lightly, cleared his throat, then said with dry sarcasm

Mulder stared at me questioningly.

"You'll have to work with Agent Dunham instead of Agent Scully. I'm sorry about that," I explained.

They exchanged a silent glance, the kind that marks the start of a shared adventure. I recognized that expression. It was the spark that joins worlds, the *Fringe Division* and the *X-Files*. They'd enjoy this collaboration.

But then Refaat erupted angrily:

"You're busy pairing them up while ignoring me completely! I refuse to work on this case!"

"Why, Doctor?" I asked, bewildered. "I thought you'd enjoy the international cooperation. Paranormal is a blast. I love it."

He gestured furiously toward them.

"Them? They know nothing about where they're standing! All they do is flashing their big guns and acting like action-movie heroes. Even our children imitate their moves better than they do!"

I sighed impatiently. "So, what you're saying, my dear Doctor Refaat, is that you'll take the case; to fix what they'll ruin."

He waved his hands dismissively. "I didn't say that. I retired. I finished my memoirs, and my adventures ended with them, by order of my creator. I can't defy him. You know how authors are. Paranormal is finished."

I leaned closer, lowering my voice. "He doesn't have to know."

Refaat blinked, half shocked, half amused.

"Are you joking? We're *inside* his world! He'll know. And besides, it's a matter of principle. I won't deceive the man who gave me life on paper."

"But these are different papers. You could call this your private practice, like leaving public service to start your own firm," I grinned cunningly.

"This case is dangerous. I read your report, and the conclusions that first came to my mind... chilled me. This case will threaten our very existence," Refaat muttered under his breath, eyes still on the corpse.

"I don't understand," I said.

"I know you don't," he replied calmly. "I'll help you until the end of today. But after that, don't look for me."

An awkward silence wrapped around the place. Then Olivia's voice broke the silence. "David, why are all these papers blank?"

I turned to her, startled. "I don't know."

Mulder pointed at the desk. "Did you examine these papers carefully yesterday?" Mulder asked me.

I thought for a moment. "No."

He smiled faintly. "There's your answer. Listen carefully: we'll never solve this mystery unless you inspect this room thoroughly, tomorrow."

"But we're inspecting it now, aren't we?" I protested.

"It must be you, alone," he said quietly. "Trust me."

"Fine," I murmured, unconvinced.

We continued our search until exhaustion claimed us all. I finally returned home, completely drained, collapsed on my bed, staring at the ceiling until sleep pulled me under.

— † —

The next morning, I sat across from Major Sam again.

"Well, David," he asked, "any progress?"

I smiled. "I came to tell you what we discovered yesterday."

He frowned. "You *already* told me yesterday what you discovered yesterday. And who's we?"

I blinked in confusion. "Me, Agent Olivia, Dr. Refaat, and Agent Fox."

He shouted, "Who?!"

"The team you assembled for me yesterday, sir," I replied weakly.

Sam rubbed his temples. "The last thing you said to me yesterday was that you needed some fresh air—which, apparently, you never got," he said in a mixture of confusion and irritation.

I glanced at the calendar on his desk. Wednesday.

"It's Wednesday," I muttered in disbelief.

"Yes," he said impatiently.

"The murder happened on Tuesday," I whispered.

"That's right," he said, now suspicious. "David, did you take any drugs?"

He was right. I had. But I didn't tell him.

So, yesterday never happened. That means I never met Mulder, Olivia, or Refaat.

It was a dream.

My lips moved softly, confirming to the real world what my mind had already concluded:

"It was a dream."

Sam sighed. "Dream, hallucination, whatever. Can you tell me about it?"

"With pleasure," I said cheerfully.

When I finished recounting the dream, he smiled in satisfaction.

"Bravo, my friend. Your subconscious is helping you, driven by your vivid imagination; to solve this strange case. You summoned two protagonists from two American TV series and one from Egyptian young adult novellas."

I thought quietly that my subconscious wouldn't have been that active without the stimulants and drugs I'd taken. It definitely had help before helping me.

"I hope it truly helps me solve this mystery," I muttered.

Then I stood up. "I'll head to the crime scene now, to see what else I can find."

"Go ahead," he said encouragingly. "Good luck."

— † —

On my way, I stopped at a café. I pulled out the papers I'd taken from the victim's desk. I preferred reading them in the open air rather than at home.

"I gazed tenderly at my three-year-old child..."

It was a short story titled *The Dagger*. I ate my breakfast as I read, and when I reached the end, I froze.

"The reader holding this story became a killer when the dagger fell into their hand. Why did you do it, you miserable person? You cannot deceive the dagger! It will find its way to you."

The story ended there.

I gulped down my coffee and rushed toward the crime scene, the story's last words echoing in my ears:

You cannot deceive the dagger. It will find its way to you.

Were those just literary words, or something real?

This was indeed a strange case.

That story was the last the writer wrote and never published. Then a thought struck me: I needed to read everything he'd ever written.

On my way, I stopped at a large bookstore and bought all seven of his published works. Flipping quickly through the pages, I skimmed each story's theme. They were all fantasies, worlds detached from reality. The man had built his own universe and lived in it, refusing to live in the real one.

That thought made me remember my own painful reality.

A headache throbbed at my temples. I pulled out a few painkillers and swallowed them, murmuring:

"Escaping into fantasy isn't so bad when reality tastes this bitter."

Then I looked ahead at the road and whispered, "God only knows what that man saw that made him build another world within this one."

I felt closer to him now.

I didn't even notice how long I'd been driving, lost in his world, until I arrived at his home. I got out of the car and entered his study. Mulder's words echoed in my mind. I knew what I have to do is to examine the room with full awareness, so that my subconscious could later retrieve what my eyes had recorded.

Hours passed.

I searched the books, the shelves, the papers, every corner of the room.

I even ordered lunch there, eating at the victim's desk, sharing, even if only for a moment, his loneliness and isolation.

When I finished, I resumed the inspection carefully, inch by inch.

And when the search was finally done, I went home, had dinner, took the stimulants and the drugs, and lay down quietly, waiting for sleep to come.

CHAPTER FOUR
SOLVING THE PUZZLE

"The words appeared on pages that were blank yesterday. Well done," Olivia said, smiling with her characteristic gentle sweetness.

"Where is Dr. Ismail?" Mulder asked suddenly.

"He left," I replied. "It seems a part of my subconscious didn't want to involve him in this."

A voice startled me. "No, my restless friend. I haven't gone anywhere," Dr. Refaat said.

I understood then that this wasn't what it seemed. His rebellious personality—the part that despised routine, life's monotony, and rigid conventions—was at play. It was the side that loved the extraordinary, the unconventional. Eventually, it would delight in joining our quest.

"You've fed your subconscious many details. The room now feels real," Mulder said in awe.

"Why do you need the room? I'm here; I can tell you everything." I frowned.

Refaat cleared his throat and pointed a finger. "It is your conscious mind that speaks. We need the information hidden in your subconscious, which your awareness cannot access."

I tilted my head. "What do you mean? I have read everything, noticed everything."

Refaat gestured to the papers scattered on the desk. "No, you haven't. You skimmed over the pages without reading the words. Your mind acted like a scanner or a photocopier, unaware of what it was recording. Now, we can read it all clearly within your subconscious. Do you see the difference?"

I was convinced. "Yes... the difference is incredible," I said nodding slowly.

Olivia cleared her throat. "Now, if you'll excuse us, we have work to do."

Refaat hungrily devoured the victim's books that he wrote, while sitting on the sofa, filling the room with a haze of tobacco smoke. Mulder began organizing the stacked books on the shelves, jotting down notes in a small notebook, while Olivia searched the desk and drawers with calm precision, examining scraps, classifying items, and reading their contents carefully.

I realized my role had ended for now. I had unleashed these literary characters from my subconscious, and they were busy exploring the memories of my mind for answers. I could finally engage fully with my consciousness, working alongside my subconscious to solve this intricate puzzle. Perhaps I could explore the rest of my mind, recall lost fragments of childhood, witness my life flash before me, encounter lost family members, or confront the suffocating darkness of nothingness.

A hand rested on my shoulder, its touch gentle, voice deep and calm. "You will find no one here."

I turned—and faced myself. I screamed in terror. "What is this? What kind of joke?"

"It's not a joke. It's you," I said calmly.

"Who are you?" I shouted at him.

"I am David," I said.

"It's me, David," I insisted.

"That's not true. I am David, and I can prove it."

"If you are David, then who am I?"

I waved my hands helplessly. "You are the mask imposed by your own defences to protect yourself from pain, to separate emotionally from others, to live alone imprisoned in your mind. You please people with your smile but harden yourself when they oppose you. You are nothing; a mere mask that pretends life is a joke, convinced that existence is imaginary and the world is a big theatre, void of truth."

"Rubbish! Pure philosophy!" I shouted.

"You wore all those masks to survive, and to forget about me," I said quietly. "I don't blame you. You couldn't endure such pain you were exposed to as a child, the pain of illness, death, abandonment, rejection, cruelty, neglect and abuse. You had to separate a part of you, convincing yourself that you are alright. That part sees your suffering self as another entity. A child cannot endure such pain. I am the wounded child within you, but I'm here, I live within you, I scream from time to time; for you to notice me and deal with me, whether in times of quiet meditation or hard times or even through your cases."

"You then represent my sad childhood, I intended to forget," I said.

"You would have died, hadn't you done that. No child can contain such psychological pain. But now, I've grown with you and became a handicap wounded child bleeding from all directions.

I recoiled, afraid. "And what do you want from me?"

"I wanted to meet you," I said softly. "I want to reconcile, to make you understand my suffering, to feel what I feel, to release the falseness."

I stepped back, trembling. "Hey! Hey! Hey! Why now, after all these years?"

"I have been trapped here since your birth in your subconscious," I said. "I was imprisoned away from everyone, from yourself," I said without getting any closer to me, feeling like a drunk, swirling around.

"But you came now," I continued in a hopeful soft voice.

"I came for the case I'm working on," I said firmly.

"By God! Isn't yourself more important than this case?" I pleaded.

"Frankly, I do not understand what you are saying," I muttered.

I sank into the background, fading, transparency increasing. Olivia approached, smiling. "This... you're from a parallel world."

"We are not in your famous series. This is me, inside my subconscious," I laughed bitterly.

"Why are there two of you here?" she asked, frowning.

"It's a long story. I don't even understand it yet," I sighed.

"Well then," she said cheerfully, "we're done. Let's exchange ideas and results. Will you join us?"

"Of course," I said quickly, moving to sit. Olivia took the sofa beside Refaat, Mulder stood tall in his famous coat, and I leaned against the desk.

"He killed himself, lady and gentlemen. I see no other explanation," Refaat spoke solemnly.

The room fell silent until I spoke. "But why are there no fingerprints?"

"Dr. Ismail never said he actually held the dagger that killed him," said Mulder as he raised his hand in a weird gesture, only he knows what it means.

"Then that dagger..." Olivia began, pausing for effect, staring at our eyes in amusement. "...was not made in this world."

"What?" I exclaimed.

"Yes," she said. "A single piece, its metallic blade, its handle of a different material, embedded with gems arising from its substance and strength."

Refaat cleared his throat. "I agree. The material doesn't exist here. It's completely an unknown alloy to us," Refaat said, waving his hands in the air, "I reached a preliminary conclusion after reading all his works; I understood the man he was."

Mulder asked curiously, "What did you understand, Dr. Ismail?"

"He faced pains too deep to mention," Refaat said. "If you gather the threads from all his stories, you see it. These pains drove him into his imagination, creating characters, events and worlds. He severed all ties with reality until he existed entirely in fantasy, writing with his hand what will lead him to his death. He never wanted to be part of his reality; he preferred joining his fictional characters more than attaching to the bitter painful reality he lived. He escaped to another universe and lived in a daydream, only he controls its elements and events."

Mulder raised his eyebrows in astonishment.

"And are there pains that can drive an educated man to such a strange life?!" he asked.

"Do not forget that he imposed upon himself a terrible solitude," Dunham said calmly, "during which he endured natural pains from his life that he could not bear, and his fertile imagination only intensified them, while his loneliness deepened."

"We do not know the amount of pain that faced that author and drove him to escape from reality," Refaat nodded in agreement, then said, "but we do know for certain that imagination exists for humans; to let them know that life exceeds the material scope they live in, and that there are spirits and an afterlife and other mysterious things they will know only in their time. Imagination has always been a motivator for development and a source of creativity; it was never meant to be a way to escape life."

"Doesn't he have something like an imaginary girl he escapes with to his own private world?" Olivia asked in wonder.

"He does not," Refaat said bitterly, "and he no longer wishes to. He has lost all faith in humanity. He is on the verge of becoming that serial killer who kills people, if not that his literature gave him the ability to do on paper what he wishes to do, without taking lives."

"He only destroyed his own soul," Mulder murmured softly.

"Then how do you explain that he killed himself?!" I asked Refaat in amazement, "A person escapes to an ideal world to rest from the fallen world he lives in."

"The answer lies in his subconscious," Refaat said. "He despaired of the entity dwelling inside him, where purity and filth, love and enmity entwine and decided to end that farce even if his consciousness did not respond."

I remembered the story of the dagger I read while awake.

"So, he built in his mind," I said, "a special dagger from resentment and unleashed it in his imaginary world, harvesting humans while safely hidden behind his pen and shielded by his books. He became that killer, but on paper. He sought nothing but blood, silent revenge, which allows him to avenge humanity in silence. But he who kills must be killed," he said inwardly. "Which led to his own death in the end."

"The dagger left his imaginary world to strike his reality," Dunham agreed, adding, "without him realizing that he was scripting his own death with his pen. He set the rules. He created a weapon that amplifies the negative emotions in people and make it real."

"Then why kill himself like that?" Mulder asked in wonder.

"He escaped life because it pained him," Refaat said, lowering his head in concentration, closer to respect, "his mind judged life as painful, and he roamed another world as a kind of escape. What he did not realize was that his mind would impose the same pain onto the fantasy, fulfilling the image embedded in him since childhood. There is no escape from the idea planted before he even knew life. His mind, to preserve its analytical and logical existence, had to achieve the equation of pain."

"So, he seeks to drink from pain that exists only in his mind," Mulder said affirmatively.

"Correct." Refaat snapped his fingers.

"All of this is fine," Dunham said thoughtfully, then asked, "but what went wrong? How does a body from the imaginary world slip into ours so easily?"

"That is a good question," I agreed.

"If the mental power that moves objects merges with the mental power that roams the subconscious during dreams, together they can bring a body from the imaginary world," Mulder said.

"But what gives that body its hidden power?" asked Dunham, "That dagger incites killing, fosters anger in hearts, and kills whoever it strikes. It is a paranormal cursed dagger. What gives it that extraordinary power?"

"The subconscious of the victim," Refaat replied.

"But it loses its power once it crosses into another world whose rules do not apply to it," I added.

"And that indeed happened. The dagger lost its strength in this world. This confirms the theory." Refaat snapped his fingers again.

"Then how did that man bring the dagger from the imaginary world so easily? How did he merge the powers of telekinesis with subconscious travel? And why bring the weapon that killed him?" I asked, feeling we were close to the solution.

Mulder said tiredly, "We already answered the last question. He could no longer bear life, which drove him to end his real life with the imaginary weapon his mind created."

"Then how did he gain that ability?" I asked

Dunham gestured in frustration,

"Look at his life. He did nothing in the present except produce literature. He did not have children, did not marry, lived alone in his home, worked isolated in his study, and only interacted with fantasies created by his mind. He would have gone mad if his imagination had not destroyed him this way."

"The question remains," I said in frustration, "how can a foreign body exit its world into ours? How did the author gain the ability to cross into his imaginary world?"

In deep voices, Refaat, Dunham, and Mulder replied respectively,

"There is a mediator."

"Search for a crosser."

"He used a carrier."

"And how can we find such a mediator?" I asked in astonishment, "The man never leaves his study!"

"You said it yourself—his study. That is his battlefield," Refaat said firmly.

"What exactly am I looking for? I only know that library contained thousands of books," I said in surprise.

"The library is useless. They are all novels, psychology, sociology, philosophy, and religion books," Mulder replied confidently.

"Look for something special, unlike the others. Something distinctive: an old, large, worn volume, an intricate artifact, papyrus sheets, carved stones. Search for a body that does not belong." Refaat said mysteriously.

"There is a large, black bound book with no title written in a strange language in the top desk drawer, and an old worn manuscript inside it, with three lines underlined," Dunham said.

Refaat stood, bringing the book and showing us.

"It's Greek. I should have expected that," said Refaat then he pointed to the three of us, saying, "there is something connecting the two worlds, the physical and the metaphysical: black magic, magical spells, demonic recitations. If we study and read this book, we may find its link to the mediators."

"Can't you read Greek?" I asked curiously.

Refaat smiled sarcastically.

"No," he said, "I can only recognize it. Remember, I am a literary figure borrowed as a projection in your subconscious, not a real person in reality."

"We solved the puzzle, gentlemen. I don't know how to thank you all," I nodded happily.

"Don't," Olivia said, as she smiled. "We are, in a way, part of you. Don't mention it. Happy to help."

Mulder held my hand strongly as he shook it. "Take that book early tomorrow and study its content," he said, "then close that strange case once you confirm the nature of this dangerous book."

I smiled. "I will," I said then waved. "Goodbye."

Olivia smiled and bowed her head in salute. Refaat nodded the other way coughing sharply, then we all vanished, plunging from my subconscious into a deep, dreamless sleep until I awoke.

CHAPTER FIVE
THE RETURN OF THE DAGGER

"Bravo, David. You've solved an impossible case," he said.

"Difficult, but not impossible, sir," I replied humbly.

He smiled, rose from his seat, walked behind me, and patted my shoulder. "You deserve praise indeed. Though I wonder how I will report this to command! Magic and objects leaving the world of imagination to enter reality and kill their creator... a story coming true."

I opened my mouth to thank him, but the phone rang first. Major Sam snatched the receiver violently and listened. A minute passed, his face darkening with every word. Then he slammed the handset into its cradle.

"What happened?!" I asked.

His mind seemed elsewhere. "Isaac... he's dead."

"How?!" I asked in astonishment.

He turned to me; disbelief etched into his features. "The dagger killed him."

He cleared his throat. "I mean, his colleague Judah stabbed him with the damned dagger."

"And how did that happen?!" I exclaimed.

He faced me, voice firm, almost commanding. "That is what we need to find out."

Handing me the report, he added, "I don't think this case is closed yet."

I took it, nodding. "I think so too." Then I left.

— † —

"I attacked him without thinking, believe me, Detective David," Judah confessed.

"You told him you were jealous, that you hated him, that he stole your spotlight, and that it was time for things to return to their proper place."

"I did."

"That was premeditated, then."

"Believe me, no. I spoke without awareness, as if my buried thoughts had overflowed violently from within."

"Those thoughts are imprisoned inside you, then, making them real."

"But my will never made them real. I never harmed Isaac, not even with a word."

"You held anger inside you, and the dagger transformed it into reality."

"But I am innocent. You know this. I never killed Isaac"

"No court or judge will accept that a still object influenced you to commit a crime. You are guilty of harbouring that hidden resentment against yourself and your colleague, in the eyes of God. Regardless, your words, the investigation reports, and the circumstances will determine your strange fate."

— † —

"Where is the dagger now, David?"

"In a secure vault under heavy guard, Major Sam."

"A vault cannot prevent it from killing. You and I both know that."

"Then let us pray that we can neutralize it before it acts."

"How can a lifeless object influence an adult?"

"That dagger, sir, cannot tell the difference between consciousness and subconscious. Its true realm is one where everything manifests. It is born of imagination. It must be destroyed here and now, or it will annihilate the entire world."

"What brought it into our world in the first place?"

"The slain author."

"And why did Judah kill Isaac?"

"Because Judah read the three lines written in the book of black magic. He awakened the dagger again, creating a new cycle of killing."

"Then let it be. Let's destroy the dagger."

"It cannot be destroyed in this world."

"Why? What protects it from fire or being crushed?!"

"My instinct says it must return to where it came from."

"And how do you plan to do that?"

"I will need to consult my extraordinary team again. I will visit my subconscious."

"Do it then, before the dagger kills again."

— † —

"Your dagger will destroy humanity if you don't close the infernal circle you began in your imagination," I shouted at him inside my subconscious.

"But the circle is already closed," he replied.

"No, clever one! You killed yourself by your hand because the circle remained open, leaving the dagger wandering for an exit."

"But the circle I made cannot be closed!"

"We will make one dead person kill another and thus end the murders."

"How?"

"Let's review your story: a father—who brought the dagger from an unknown source—kills his son due to financial strain, then buries the dagger in muddy earth. A man with a dog finds it and kills the father, seeking revenge, for what the father did to his father, then throws the dagger into the Eastern Riverbank. The nephew of the killer finds it in the Eastern Riverbank on the ferry, kills his uncle with it to gain his wealth, leaves his uncle to burn in an oven with the dagger, and then a girl kills him for honour when she finds the dagger in bread. Her jealous colleague kills her in the restroom after taking the dagger from a forensic lab worker, throwing it into a drain. A random killer finds it, murders with it, throws it through a window, and a son kills his mother with it."

The author, whom I found somehow awake and alive inside his study, while I saw neither Refaat, Olivia, nor Fox— perhaps they had done their part perfectly—acknowledged:

"That is correct."

"The dagger fulfilled its role until the murderer gave it to the child. It was meant for the child to murder the random killer, not his mother. That disrupted the sequence, leaving your story in limbo. You ruined the murderous loop at the very end. Your silent rage toward your parents and society shaped your imagination. Now the dagger should kill both the random murderer and the child, not just the child. To resolve this, the dagger acted in your stead instead of the child."

"What? What do you mean?!"

"You saw yourself as the child who killed his mother, the source of existence, the suppression of individuality, the pain of isolation replacing the joy of intimate connection. So, the dagger voluntarily killed you to close the loop."

"But the murderer remains."

"Exactly. And he killed Judah."

"But Isaac killed Judah."

"In reality, the murderer did. He now drives the bloody dagger in the real world."

"You made the dagger to kill autonomously."

I said, with a harshness I didn't truly feel:

"And it did. But the murderer killed you—the author—in your symbolic child form, then was freed to kill Isaac, opening a new circle in a new world, observing events like watching an 8 o'clock drama, safe from harm, just as you did when you created their dark world."

He admitted with pain, "The dark world I joined."

"You joined it willingly in your imagination, but they pulled you in against your will."

"What do you want me to do?" he asked, surrendering.

"The only solution is to kill the murderer in the imaginary world and leave the dagger there after it kills you."

"The dagger's effect will remain in reality, and it will kill Judah by another hand."

"If you close your story's circle, the dagger will find no escape from your imagined world. Remember, you are already dead. We will burn the book of black magic in reality and pray it ends there. You created the dagger, gave it evil power, left the child and the murderer, then the murderer killed the child in his symbolic form as you as I told you, and now all you need is to kill the murderer."

"If this is what you wish, I will do it. But how do we bring the dagger into your subconscious from reality?"

"The same way you drew it from imagination into reality."

He spoke as if he'd solved a puzzle: "The three lines... wait, I'll bring the book."

"I wish it so," I murmured.

He read the three lines, and the dagger appeared in his hand.

"How will I track the murderer while in your subconscious?" the author asked.

We went to the desk, and I handed him the papers. "He is inside these sheets. He killed you when he threw the dagger through them into your world. I think you know how to bring it from your imagination to kill him in my subconscious."

"Wait, I'll try."

He plunged the dagger into the papers over the desk— once, twice, ten times—until the sheets tore into a thousand pieces. Dark red blood flowed, a hand emerged, stretching, growing until the elbow, shoulder, and head appeared. Its other arm crawled over the desk until it fell. Before his complete form emerged from the torn papers, the author struck his heart three times. His movements ceased entirely, though a mocking smile lingered, wrapped in insanity. The author's creation had been utterly mad, the source of chaos in his nightmarish story.

I hoped it would end like this.

The author smiled kindly, then shook my hand. "It is over now."

"I hope so. You succeeded," I said.

"I am the projection of the author inside your mind, who managed to bring the dagger here and end the chaotic fantasy it caused," he said humbly.

"I am glad you helped, even if you aren't real," I said excitedly.

"I apologize for the problems I caused," he said sadly.

"It's us who should apologize for failing to help you. I know somehow it was your subconscious, not your consciousness, that killed you. Civil authorities should have felt your pain and aided you," I said, in real grief.

He shook his head in regret. "What difference does it make? I killed myself anyway. Remember, I am the author's subconscious speaking to you within your subconscious."

Then, tenderly: "If you truly want to help me, help yourself. Your life is in ruins too. I fled from reality to imagination, while you fled to work. Yet heaven's mercy did not abandon you; You met me, and your suffering self, within your subconscious. Perhaps you should start caring for yourself, give yourself some tender, care and love."

"I thank you, my dear friend," I said, moved.

He nodded respectfully. "Farewell, my friend."

I knew I would miss that gentle soul I never had the honour to meet in reality, regretting his departure within my subconscious and not meeting him in reality, I whispered my own farewell.

CHAPTER SIX
THE DETECTIVE'S CASE

"You've closed the case this time for real, David. The dagger has vanished from the iron vault; there is no trace of it, everything has returned to how it was, and we've completed two operations after the dagger case," Major Sam said, smiling as he continued.

"I officially closed the case and accepted the strange report you wrote. Command has decided to grant you an exceptional bonus and promotion."

My smile widened, then I straightened in my seat. "Of course, I appreciate that, sir, but I need something else."

He looked at me, curious. I replied firmly, "A vacation... a long one."

His gaze pierced me. "David, we are friends before colleagues. This case—it's different, isn't it?"

I nodded sincerely. "Yes, it certainly is different."

"In what way?" he asked with intense curiosity.

I said with conviction, "It drew my attention to a larger case, one I've decided to devote a great deal of attention to from now on."

"What case?" he pressed, almost breathless with curiosity.

I said with firmness, "Myself."

"You?!" he exclaimed in utter astonishment.

"Yes," I confirmed. "The case is me, the one I intend to care for in the coming days. I want to reconcile with myself. I've been estranged from myself since the beginning of my existence, and my conflict with myself is what has made my life miserable."

I lowered my head. "For the first time in over thirty years, during the dagger case, I met myself. He is suffering and in need of care, and I will look after him."

Major Sam said, concerned, "For a moment, your words sound like nonsense."

Then, smiling, he continued, "But I understand what you mean. Believe me, we are all on the same boat heading for hell, drugged by life itself instead of steering toward an island of bliss. Well done, my friend, for changing course. I hope you reach your destination safely."

I gripped his hand. "Thank you, my friend. I'll be back soon."

He patted my shoulder. "I'll wait for your return eagerly."

— † —

Steam rose from the ink of the book, and the words ignited in crimson flames, melting the paper like wax in a circular patch at the centre of the book. Soon, a blue icy layer formed where the melted wax had been, freezing the scene for a moment. Then a sharp tip of a metal weapon pierced the centre of the ice, climbing upward, melting it as it glowed like a thousand suns, quivering and surging, bright and furious.

When the blade finally emerged fully from the book, it hesitated for three seconds, then struck the chest of the stunned person sitting in front of the book, sinking until the hilt was buried in flesh. Only then did everything return to normal: the papers and ink restored, the steam vanished, the dagger's glow extinguished, leaving behind an ordinary metal weapon.

The man at the desk screamed, yet without moving a muscle. He spoke without a single hair trembling, pleading:

"Save me, David."

I stood there, yet I wasn't truly present, as if the wind and I were one, roaming freely like spirits. I had no ability to speak, though I tried.

A shirtless man with matted hair, torn clothes, and blood that is not his, flowing from every part of him leapt from the pages. He looked around like a primitive insecure, wild creature, eyes flashing with feral desire, then turned to the slain figure who had just called to me:

"You. Get a life. You've immersed yourself in fantasy to such an extent that your life in reality seems imaginary. You walk the streets doubting everything—your existence, gravity, the existence of people around you, the purpose of your actions, the meaning of life. But here with us, you doubt nothing. You play with your mind wherever, whenever, however you wish, being as you dream, acting as you desire, scheming plots, solving puzzles, traversing skies, weaving events, linking hearts. You are in your original world. You cannot leave us so easily."

Then, pointing at the dagger with madness:

"I've made you, against your will, part of our world—our world that you created."

He struck his chest with his right fist, exclaiming, "What you killed with the dagger were thoughts, and thoughts do not die. Thoughts do not die. Only you can die."

He lifted his head high. "I do not."

He laughed, mad and unrestrained. I circled him softly, hovered beside his right eye, then ascended behind his left arm, flying toward the slain figure. I spiralled around the dagger several times, then around the victim, and finally circled the entire scene. The victim's thoughts penetrated my undefined being:

"Kill him, David. Kill him, my dear. I need you. Kill him."

I observed the scene and understood I had been here before. I was dreaming. It was the same case. I saw a pen moving from the victim's hand toward the pages from which the dagger emerged. When it struck, it exploded, releasing shards of ink that formed the killer, who then plunged a dagger into the victim-author's chest. A different version of the same essence emerged in this new dream.

The victim's blood gushed as the dagger shot forward like a projectile, striking with its hilt the murderer, flinging him backward, drenching him in blood. The blood crept across the floor, the desk, the bookshelf, the furniture, and the walls, flowing toward me insistently. The entire scene turned crimson.

I tried to open my mouth to scream, but I had no mouth. I tried to open my eyes to wake but had none. I tried to strike myself to awaken but had no hands. Rage and rebellion surged through my veins like an erupt volcano, until I awoke, drenched in sweat, adrenaline coursing through me in extreme anger and excitement. I drank some water and returned to sleep.

— † —

"Good evening, my dear," I said on the phone to my former fiancée.

"Good evening, David. Everything alright?" she replied.

"I need a favour," I said directly.

There was a pause, so I quickly added to ease her mind:

"I'm not asking you to come back to me, out of respect for your free will, I only ask for your help."

"What kind of help?" she asked, her tone slightly stern.

"I need to visit a prisoner and two children," I said, hesitant.

She laughed softly. "Sounds like social work to me."

"Yes, it is," I confirmed.

"Will you come?" she asked, playful.

"For that, someone else was created, my dear... a helper to assist," she added, in a tone tinged with women's rights advocacy. "An equal."

It was her weekly day off, and the request touched her heart, and the requester was once dear to her, which pushed her to say, "come by in an hour."

"I will," I said eagerly.

When I arrived and sounded the horn, she took her seat next to me in the car. She asked, uncertain, "Who is the prisoner we are visiting?"

"My brother," I replied quickly.

"And why do you want me with you?" she asked candidly.

"To support me emotionally. I haven't seen him since he entered prison. I fear meeting him as much as I long to; I need you by my side."

"I can be your friend today, David," she said, moved.

After completing the visit procedures, I saw my brother and froze. Then I broke down, crying, releasing all the bottled-up emotions I had stored since childhood. Between sobs, I said:

"Forgive me, brother. I separated my feelings from you to avoid pity, to avoid being affected by you, to feel superior. The easiest way to feel superior is to belittle others. In your case, all I had to do was remain silent, leaving you to suffer as you are, without help from those closest to you."

I touched in him the author's sadness as he tapped his head. "Take it easy, brother. We all have our struggles. You too, as I remember, suffered."

"But I chose to isolate myself from you and the world, to protect myself from future pain or old memories, while you faced your pain alone without support," I said, in anguish.

My fiancée bit her lower lip, eyes glistening with emotion. She patted my shoulder for support, then held it firmly, gently encouraging.

"Listen, David. I am overjoyed to see you since you entered this door. I don't care about what you said. I'm just happy you came, brother," he continued in an uplifting tune.

I looked at him affectionately. He continued:

"But I'm also happy that you opened your heart to me, sharing what's inside. This is a real meeting, brother—not a casual greeting of 'good morning, how's it going? Good weather, bad traffic, see you later' or small talk. I meet you now, truly, for the first time since we were children."

"I am glad for this meeting, brother," I said, smiling.

He cleared his throat awkwardly, noticing my fiancée. "You didn't introduce me to your partner!"

I glanced at him, puzzled. Before I could respond, she said:

"I am his fiancée."

I noticed a change in her—feelings resurfaced, a flutter toward me. I couldn't resist stealing glances at her during the half-hour I spent speaking with my brother. When the visit ended, she said quietly in the car:

"You didn't tell me you'd be like this!"

"What do you mean?" I asked, surprised.

"You were vibrant, alive, open to others; your inner self was no longer separated from your outer," she said, astonished.

I reflected on the case I faced with my own defences separating me from my true self and said calmly:

"It's a psychological awakening—a return to the self."

"Do you do this with everyone?" she exclaimed.

"Of course not. Only with my small circle of close relationships. Not at work."

I stopped the car, pointing to two children playing in a kindergarten. "These are my children," I said warmly.

I leapt out, ran to them; they ran to me, embracing me together. I carried them to my fiancée. "I want you to meet someone very dear to your father," I said.

We played and laughed together, the time flying past. When I drove them home, I then took my fiancée along, who said:

"It was a very special day."

"Indeed, it was. I don't know how to thank you," I said.

"You surprised me! I've never seen you like this! You were someone different from what I knew."

I frowned. "It is the real me you saw today—or a glimpse of him. I plan to get to know myself again, the person I used to be, buried within me."

"I want to know him too," she said enthusiastically.

"What? Wait! I never intended to influence you," I said, astonished.

"You didn't," she assured me.

"Don't take us home; go anywhere else," she added softly.

"Of course, my dear. Anywhere you wish," I said.

I drove toward the road ahead forward.

— † —

Cairo, 13/10/2010

ACKNOWLEDGMENT

Some shadows linger longer than others. The worlds of mystery, paranormal, and human struggle have left their mark here, shaping the paths of those who walk these pages.

Dagger includes respectful references to characters from *The X-Files*, *Fringe*, and *Paranormal*. These characters belong to their original creators, and their presence here serves only as a tribute to the imagination and vision that have inspired generations of readers.

To those who wander these pages, thank you for letting these shadows accompany you.

A NOTE TO THE READER

Thank you for reading. This is a shared space of imagination and presence, where thought and feeling meet. I appreciate your presence here. Without it, the message would not reach.

AUTHOR'S NOTE

1440, *Woman*, and *Dagger* were originally written in Arabic in 2005, 2009, and 2010 respectively, and later translated into English by the author in 2025 and 2026. The original texts have been preserved as faithfully as possible, honouring the time, language, and context in which they were written.

1440 is a reflection on the quiet power of time and the unseen impact of presence. Through a series of interconnected encounters, the novel explores attention, consequence, and the subtle weight of human existence, revealing how ordinary moments shape lives through brief decisions, silent kindness, and the choice to pause.

Woman examines the tension between tenderness and aggression, vulnerability and dominance. It explores the pain of both the one who wounds and the one who is wounded, where love is withheld, needs remain unmet, and rejection reshapes the heart. Through psychological and philosophical inquiry, the novel invites reflection on acceptance, responsibility, and the demanding nature of love.

Dagger moves through shadows both seen and unseen, exploring fear, choice, and the hidden corners of the human mind. It is a cautionary tale of pain, awareness, and the possibility of redemption, where even the darkest paths may reveal insight for those who dare to walk them.

Written across twenty-one years and two languages, these works trace a personal and philosophical journey through time, memory, and the evolving consciousness of the author. Together, they form an integrated exploration of presence, identity, and moral awareness, moving from quiet observation to emotional inquiry, to confrontation with darkness and the possibility of redemption. This volume presents these works as they were conceived, without revision or modernisation.

ABOUT THE AUTHOR

Eddie Mikhail is an engineer and novelist whose work explores psychology, philosophy, and the inner lives of his characters. His writing often blends realism with symbolic and introspective elements, examining emotional conflict between inner experience and lived reality through layered narrative structures. Across his novels, he approaches fiction as a space for questioning rather than resolution, allowing ambiguity and reflection to guide the reader's experience. His stories illuminate the hidden corners of the mind and heart, exploring presence, identity, morality, and the subtle forces that shape human experience.

Born in Egypt in 1983, Eddie wrote his first novel in 2002 and completed his Bachelor of Engineering in 2004. He originally wrote his early works in Arabic and later translated them into English, bringing his stories to new readers while preserving their original intent and context. He now resides in NSW, Australia, continuing to write, reflect, and explore the inner workings of the human mind and human behaviour.

CONNECT WITH THE AUTHOR

Postal Address:
PO Box 737
Campbelltown NSW 2560
Australia
Website: https://thewordconnects.com
Email: thewordconnects@outlook.com